THE
Finest Tree

and other
Christmas Stories
from Atlantic Canada

edited by Dan Soucoup

NIMBUS
PUBLISHING LTD

Nimbus Publishing Limited
3731 Mackintosh St, Halifax, NS B3K 5A5
(902) 455-4286 nimbus.ca

Printed and bound in Canada

NB1132

Interior design: Jenn Embree
Cover design: Heather Bryan

"Belsnickles—Vanishing Race" republished with permission from The Halifax Herald Ltd.

"Feeding the Family" reprinted with permission from Hilda Chaulk Murray, *More Than 50%: Woman's Life in a Newfoundland Outport, 1900–1950* (St. John's: Flanker Press, 2013), 181–84.

Josie Penny: "A Joyous Winter" originally appeared in *So Few On Earth: A Labrador Métis Woman Remembers*; (Dundurn Press, 2010) with permission of Dundurn Press.

Library and Archives Canada Cataloguing in Publication

The finest tree : and other Christmas stories from Atlantic Canada / edited by Dan Soucoup.
ISBN 978-1-77108-170-2 (pbk.)
1. Christmas stories, Canadian (English)—Atlantic Provinces. 2. Christmas—Atlantic Provinces. I. Soucoup, Dan, 1949-, editor

PS8237.C57F55 2014   C813'.0108334   C2014-903192-0

Nimbus Publishing acknowledges the financial support for its publishing activities from the Government of Canada through the Canada Book Fund (CBF) and the Canada Council for the Arts, and from the Province of Nova Scotia through Film & Creative Industries Nova Scotia. We are pleased to work in partnership with Film & Creative Industries Nova Scotia to develop and promote our creative industries for the benefit of all Nova Scotians.

THE
Finest Tree

Contents

CHRISTMAS MEMORIES

Introduction

The origins of the Christmas story go back many centuries, but Charles Dickens's masterpiece, *A Christmas Carol*, certainly took the genre to a different level by popularizing the whole notion of kindness and good cheer among people—especially at Christmas. Since everyday life for so many people in early Victorian England had turned bleak and dreary with industrialization, Dickens's little story of the joys of charity and giving around the traditional December holiday surely struck a cord with readers.

Released just days before Christmas in 1843, sales of *A Christmas Carol* were so brisk that the first print run sold out immediately, with the second and third printings quickly following. And for a number of years after, a new Dickens Christmas story became a much sought-after treasure by the reading public. But nothing would surpass the popularity and influence of *A Christmas Carol*. In fact many of the holiday traditions portrayed in the short novel became essential elements of any respectable Victorian family's Christmas celebrations, including carol-singing, plum pudding, mince pies, and turkey dinner. In fact the latter became such a Christmas stable in Victorian England after the publication of *A Christmas Carol* that the established tradition of cooking a Christmas goose was almost no more.

In North America the Dickensian world of Tiny Tim, Cratchit, and Scrooge became equally popular, so much so that within four days of *A Christmas Carol*'s arrival on a Boston wharf, pirated editions were being hawked on the streets for as little as six cents a copy. British North America also adopted Dickens's first Christmas novel as the quasi-official depiction of a classic Christmas, and many of our cherished holiday traditions in Atlantic Canada are based on celebrations described in Dickens's small book.

In this new Atlantic Canadian Christmas collection, storyteller David Goss has traced the very beginnings of these early holiday celebrations in pre-Confederation British North America and reports on the influence of Dickens and others on the celebrations of Christmases past in the Atlantic region. The history of Victorian military Christmas traditions on Citadel Hill in downtown Halifax is the subject of another fascinating story by Trudy Duivenvoorden Mitic. And not to be outdone, broadcaster and writer Norman Creighton has given an outstanding account of the history of sending Christmas greetings in Maritime Canada by means of horse and buggy, snowshoe, toboggan, canoe, and even the occasional iceboat.

The Finest Tree also includes a number of treasured Christmas stories from some of the region's most celebrated writers, including Lucy Maud Montgomery, Ernest Buckler, Alden Nowlan, Beatrice MacNeil, Gary L. Saunders, and David Weale. While not all stories are happy—Alden Nowlan in particular paints a stark but realistic picture of rural poverty years ago—they are all, without doubt, powerful and engaging, contributing to our understanding of Atlantic Canadian Christmases in days gone by.

Storytelling is one of the most enduring expressions of a rich cultural life and nowhere is this more evident than in Atlantic Canada at Christmastime. Hopefully this little collection will cheer and inspire readers in some small way, perhaps as the work of the great Dickens did many decades ago.

—*Dan Soucoup*

Christmas Stories

One Happy Christmas

ELSIE DOUGLAS VANWART

Set in New Brunswick's York County in the early 1900s, Elsie Douglas VanWart's tale takes place in a simpler time, when snowstorms at Christmas were considered delightful and sleigh rides through the countryside were everyday occurrences.

It had been snowing softly all day. The year of the "big snow," 1914, had already begun in earnest. In some places the snow, even now, was high above our heads, but we children, Claire, my two small brothers, and myself, loved every bit of it.

Today, we were especially happy, because soon Daddy would be coming home, and, tonight after supper we all (all except Mother that is) were going to drive into the village to the Sunday school Christmas tree party. Daddy had promised last night.

We had never seen Mother as happy as she was that winter. Staying, as we were, temporarily, in her old home in the country, we often surprised her in her "remembering look" (as we called it), especially when she found a moment to sit down on the old rocking chair by the back window in the kitchen. She could look out on the orchard there, the fields and the woods beyond. She had been smiling too, this morning as Dad had driven off, all bundled up in the pung with a fur robe over his knees, and he called out: "See you this afternoon—be good"; and Old Ted, our horse, had taken him on the trot down the long stretch to the gate, and out on to the main road.

My father was not a big man, only tall, but as he kissed us goodbye that morning, dressed as he was in his big beaver-skin coat, with mittens and cap to match, he looked immense. We laughed, and some of us even tried on his big mittens with the leather palms. They felt lovely and warm, but of course were much too big for our small hands. His cap, really a hat when the ear-tabs were tied up, he wore on top of his head, and when he was happy, as he was today, it gave him a very jaunty look. We noticed, however, before he got even as far as the gate, the ear-tabs had been pulled down. It was snowing some, and there was a sharpness in the air.

We watched him out of sight, secretly wishing we might have gone along, too, but Mother had suggested that since we were all to be up so late tonight, we should stay home and have an afternoon nap.

It was not hard, though, for us to picture Dad as he drove along, for we had gone with him many times before. He was a lumberman and would be making the rounds of his logging camps. This had been a very good winter for the cutting and hauling of logs.

Now, if spring did not come too early, he had high hopes for a good "cut" and expected to have all in readiness for the spring drive. The logs piled with precision along the banks of the Nashwaak River would then be pushed off into the water and (with the aid of freshets farther up, and men called stream drivers) floated down to the millpond. There the logs would be caught in a gigantic boom, from which they would be drawn up into the mill and sawn into boards, laths, shingles, and firewood. The little village of Stanley would hum all summer with the sound of my father's sawmill.

At least we'd likely have saved ourselves a tumble into the deep snow today! It was getting to be a joke with the lumberjacks, for often as not, as we drove swiftly over the iced lumber roads, (Dad usually singing at the top of his voice and we children joining in), we'd forget, momentarily, that we might meet up with a load of logs, or the watering cart itself that was used to make them icy. Suddenly we'd come upon a team hauling its big load, and turning-out places being few and far between, we'd charge into a snowdrift to let them pass, and over would go the pung on its side, and we'd spill in all directions. What a scramble we'd have until we were all safely tucked in again. Luckily, Old Ted was a quiet creature, and we'd always make camp. And then the food! The quantities of it that cook would put before us. Even the slight tarpaper taste that always remained on any we brought home with us was never detected while there.

But today we did not have time for so much thinking. Hadn't Daddy said it would be nice, if on his return he found a path shovelled from the house to the barn? We did do the shovelling. We even filled the big wood box by the stove in the kitchen for Mother; and after our rest we had time to play all afternoon with our sleds and snowshoes. The snowshoes were our pride and joy. They even had a coat of varnish and we loved, too, the coloured tufts of wool around their edges. Why, we could even walk on top of the line fence with them this winter!

We were playing happily, but relieved, too, when Mother called for us to come in. The days were very short now, and the storm had hastened the night. It had definitely turned colder. Our hands and feet had begun to feel numb under our warm, thick clothing.

We ran up on the veranda in front of the house and had fun brushing the snow off one another with a broom that was always kept there for that purpose.

Mother, looking very fresh in a pale blue dress, was ready at the door. She stood back a little so as not to get the full blast of the cold we brought in with us. She took our coats as we took them off, and hung each in turn on its peg near the shed door. She had our bedroom slippers ready and we took off our rubbers, oversocks and high boots as well, placing them by the stove so that they would be warm and dry for tonight's outing.

As we did this Mother moved about the big, warm kitchen preparing supper. The aroma from the oven was tantalizing. We were having corn cake (we children always referred to it as johnnycake) with maple syrup for dessert. A very special treat. The kitchen seemed even cozier than usual tonight, with the sound of the dry wood crackling and burning in the big stove, the red lights that played through the now open grates, and the tea kettle bubbling away on the top of the stove.

We washed by the sink, taking turns pumping the hand pump for the water. This Mother warmed for us by pouring a little hot water from the teakettle into the basin. We girls brushed our hair and helped each other with the hair-ribbon bows that sat on top of our heads like butterflies. We loved their perkiness and bright red colour. The boys plastered their hair down with a wet brush and were very independent about it, climbing up on a chair to view themselves in the mirror hanging above the sink.

Now we were ready. We all crowded on the couch in front of the big kitchen window which faced the road and up which Daddy should soon be coming. The couch, a lovely old mahogany one, had seen much use, and really looked out of place in a kitchen. It had belonged to our great-great-grandmother. She had brought it out from England with her when she came as a bride, and it must have looked even more out of place in the little log cabin where she had first set up house.

The horsehair covering was worn prickly but we did not mind that tonight. We each, with our fingers, made little holes in the frosted window to peep through, and then sat there watching patiently.

It was snowing hard now, and blowing a little colder too, and there was a white frost all around the door we had just come in. On the inside though, the kitchen itself was very warm. We were quiet for a moment. You could even hear Tabby the cat, stretched out behind the stove, purring. She knew all the warmest spots.

Rusty, our big brown-and-white collie dog, who had come in soon after we did, lay snoring on the hooked rug by the front door. With his thick coat he had instinctively chosen a cooler spot. With one ear cocked, even in sleep, he seemed to sense he was on guard and must be ready, at the first sound of sleigh bells, to run to greet his master.

Mother was now setting the table in the kitchen. It was much too cold to eat in the dining room tonight. It had a northern exposure, and the wind was blowing from the northwest. We were pleased, though, to hear her going into the cold room several times to get the things she loved using while here, like the old pewter salts and peppers, and a dear little mustard pot, lined with deep blue glass. The jug she was now bringing out for the maple syrup was very old, too, and we children loved pouring from it. Our aunt, whose house it now was, had a cruet-stand for the centre of the table for holding all those things but we, like Mother, preferred the pewter.

The old upright clock on the mantle ticked away the minutes, but still there was no sign of Daddy. We began to get restless and I could see that Mother, each time she passed the window, cast an anxious look towards the road.

"Come, children come," she said at last, "we'll start supper. Your dad should be along any minute now."

She could no longer bear the look of disappointment that was beginning to show on our faces. We were almost in tears. Even the thought of our special dessert could not down the fear that Daddy might not get home in time; that he might not take us to the Christmas tree party, after all. Even if he did come soon, would he want to start out again in this storm? Would Old Ted be too tired to go over the road again?

We took our places at the table reluctantly. For Claire and myself, on the far side, it wasn't too bad: we could still look out the window. But for our small brothers, with their backs to the window, it was a different story. They kept wiggling around in their chairs so much that Mother fully expected to see their whole supper land on her nice clean floor.

Suddenly, we heard a bell! We jumped! Telephones were new that winter, and expecting to hear the soft tinkle of sleigh bells, the harsh sound, right in our ears, startled us for a moment.

As Mother took up the receiver to answer it now, we all listened with apprehension. We could not hear all that was said, but we could tell it was Daddy's voice. (He still felt he must yell into "the thing," as he called it!)

We heard Mother say: "All fine, all fine here. But where are you?"

"Oh!"

"No."

"When?"

"Which camp?"

"What does the doctor say?"

"Yes."

"That's good."

"Oh yes!"

"Of course not. They are all here in the kitchen with me now—and listening."

"Good. But what about yourself and Old Ted?"

"All right. I'll get the children ready."

We began to relax; began to breathe again. It looked as if some how we were still going to be able to go. We could hardly keep from calling out, but Mother, still at the phone, went on:

"Yes."

"No."

"Well, then, you'll be able to get a good rest tomorrow. I am so glad you do not have to disappoint the children."

"Yes. Oh! Has it stopped?" She glanced out the back window.

"Yes, it has stopped here too, I hadn't noticed."

"Yes, I saw the men go by with the plough about an hour ago."

"No, our road has not seemed to fill in too much this storm."

"All right."

"Goodbye."

Mother turned the little handle at the side of the phone, ring-ing off, then she turned to us and said: "That was your father. He's coming.

"One of the men at the Mick Road Camp cut his foot with an axe. Your father had to take him to the doctor. The doctor says he'll be all right now. He says for everyone to be dressed and ready before he comes. He'll just have time to give Ted his oats, and have a quick supper himself. Luckily the storm is over and the road ploughed.

"Now, let me see, Elsie, you run up to the spare room and get your Sunday dresses, I laid them out on the bed; Claire, you look in your bottom bureau drawer and get a pair of extra socks. If you are going to sit in behind on the floor of the pung, you'll need extra clothing, even with the straw your father put on the floor this morning.

"Turning to the boys, she said: "Andy, do you suppose you and Stan could carry that bundle of blankets I left in the hall, out here to the couch? We must have everything ready."

The happy squeals of preparation were still going on when Daddy drove in at the gate—the distance between us and the village was only two miles, but to us then, of course, it seemed much farther.

We really hurried now, and by the time Daddy came walking up the path from the barn, we were all—including Rusty—on the veranda to greet him and brush him off. He was carrying a pail, which he handed to Andy, saying "Good! I see you boys are all dressed and ready. Do you suppose you could manage to take some water out to Old Ted? I left him eating his oats, but the water in the puncheon at the barn is frozen solid. I left the lighted lantern hanging in the stable, so it won't be dark."

They went off with much laughing and spilling, glad to be "little men" for Daddy, and glad, too, to have something to do while they waited. Rusty, barking furiously, followed after them. The rest of us went back into the house, and soon Daddy was sitting down to his hot supper. As he ate, he eyed us, dressed in our old winter coats, but proudly wearing the red caps and mittens Mother had made for us. He looked at us again, and then winked at Mother.

"It's real cold out, Maggie! Frosty too!"

Mother hesitated, then smiled and left the room. We heard her going towards the old parlour and opening the door; we heard her catch her breath with the cold, for it had been closed off since Sunday. We were not too surprised when she came out, closing the door behind her, to see that she was carrying a big brown paper parcel.

While in the parlour on Sunday, singing carols, we had peeked behind the organ, but we refrained from mentioning that fact now. We watched Mother set the parcel on the table opposite to where

Daddy was eating, and untie the cord. We had peeked, but we were scarcely prepared for the surprise that now met our eyes.

There they were, two beautiful Astrakhan fur collars, more like capes, with another collar attached at the neck, which could be turned up to keep the ears warm when it was windy or cold. We danced for joy; we hugged each parent in turn, thanking them over and over again, and almost overthrowing them completely. We then proceeded to put on our wonderful gifts. It was our turn now to stand up on a chair and peer before the mirror over the sink. We strutted around the kitchen like young peacocks!

We knew that this was our Christmas for this year, come early, but we did not mind. We'd still be able to share in our brothers' gifts (they were so hoping for a toboggan, but so far there was no sign of it behind the organ!)—however, to have ours now, to wear tonight, made us feel so warm, so loved, and even the shivers of excitement that had been going up and down our spines all day seemed calmed. We were very warm indeed, both inside and out.

Soon we were all ready. As we said goodbye, Daddy looked at Mother with concern and said: "Sure you're all right, Mother? I hate to leave you alone like this. I do wish you were able to come along, too."

"I'll be fine, dear," she answered.

"I'll have Tabby and Rusty to keep me company—and with the phone right here in the kitchen…."

(I know now why Mother did not venture out that cold winter's night!) Turning to us she said: "I'll stay home and tend the fires and have everything nice and warm for you when you get back."

We were off. Dad's hazel eyes were again sparkling. His look sometimes was not so much like Mother's "remembering look" but rather one of satisfaction, at being able to give us, his children, some of the "little extras" of life.

I well remember his saying once: "I want you children to have very happy memories of your childhood." He certainly succeeded in that. (His parents, though they gave to him and to his two sisters all the advantages of a good education, had worked so very hard themselves in the big country store which they owned in the village, that they had had very little time or energy left over to play with their small family.)

We loved driving this road in the winter. When we could get Old Ted to trot over the "thank-you-mums," as we called the little hills on the road made by the drifting snow, it felt much the same as when we swung high on the big swing in the barn.

We were soon entering the village, and as we turned into the rectory, halfway down the big hill to the village proper, we wished it were light so that we could see the village itself nestled there between the two hills, with the frozen river between, and the covered bridge over which we'd have to go to get to the other side. It must be a picture tonight, we thought, under this mantle of fresh snow!

Dad tied Old Ted up in the shelter by the church, and soon we were gingerly making our way, walking in fresh footsteps, on the narrow path that had been shovelled earlier. We could hear the sound of happy, excited voices, and as we entered the porch we got a glimpse of a lighted room with a big green tree standing in the corner.

There were many happy greetings and we were soon being deluged with questions about "How do you like living in the country this winter?"

"Where did you get those beautiful fur capes?"

But we did not have long to chat, for the voice of a man behind us, as we waited before a closed door, in the hall, said: "Hello! Hello children! I have just come down that chimney out there in the kitchen— watch now I'm all over soot!"

Sure enough, there he was, old Santa himself! Our eyes fairly popped and when he opened the door and led us into the next room, our joy was beyond description.

There it was, the tree we had seen through the window, but now it was a "magic tree." It was simply covered with small, lighted candles, in candleholders, and being cautiously watched over by our Sunday school teachers. There were other decorations, too, like long strings of coloured popcorn, tinsel, red paper bells, and a big shining star on top. Besides, literally covering the whole tree, were dozens of small parcels, small white parcels, that made it look like the trees out of doors when they are laden with snow; the candle-light playing on the crumpled white tissue paper made us think of when the sun comes out after a storm and shines on the snow and makes it sparkle.

We sang carols until the candles burned down. Only when each candle was carefully snuffed out were the big oil lamps brought in, and the fun of giving out the parcels began. No one was forgotten, and it seemed no time at all until we were having our hot chocolate, and then putting on our outer clothing for the homeward journey.

Maybe it's only a nostalgic memory, but it did seem as though Dad, as he climbed into the sleigh, smiled a little like old Santa did, as he passed so close to us in the hall. And the sleigh bells, as they again began their rhythmic tune, caused by the motion of our going, they, too, sounded somehow like the bells old Santa had worn around his big middle and that had tinkled every time he laughed.

As we drove along now (we were much too bundled up to look sideways!), the road ahead looked like yards and yards of shiny rib-bon. The storm was over, and the moon peeping out from behind the still-dark clouds made, for us sleepy children, a veritable fairyland of pure whiteness. It did seem such a short time before we were turning in at our own gate and Old Ted was pulling us slowly up the long stretch to the house.

Yes there was Mother, silhouetted in the window. Rusty had climbed up on the couch to look out too. We were back home again. We had managed to go to the party after all. Our safe little world was all wrapped snugly around us. We were very sleepy. We were content.

The Finest Tree

ERNEST BUCKLER

*Ernest Buckler weaves a captivating story set at Christmas in 1940s
Nova Scotia. While young Nova Scotians are dying at the front in Italy,
those back home are desperately attempting to stay calm and celebrate
the small pleasures of Christmas.*

"**B**ut Kate," I said, "aren't you going to have a tree? Don't think
I feel it will not be different this year, but...."

"No," my wife replied. "Please. It's no use."

Her face had that little paleness about the mouth, which had
been there ever since the day Nick went away, as if she were cold.

"This business of forcing yourself to do the same things as if
nothing had happened, I don't see it. Something has happened. It
hasn't anything to do with being brave. Dick, honestly, I could be
brave enough if there was any sense in putting on that kind of show.

"I haven't cried," she added, almost defiantly. "Even when I was
alone."

I knew that was true. That day when I came back into the house,
the day our son had finished his last leave, she had not turned from
the window. She had just said, "Was the train crowded?"

The voice I shall not forget. But I knew she had not been crying.

I didn't quite know what to say now. I had never seen Katherine like this, and it made me a little afraid. Apparently she mistook my hesitation.

"Oh, Dick," she cried suddenly, "please don't *make* me do it."

"Darling," I said, "whatever gave you the idea I wanted to make you do it? Anyway, perhaps you're right. Perhaps it *would* be better if we pretend it's just another Saturday."

She seemed to relax. This was the second day before Christmas, the day we always did get the Christmas tree when Nick was home.

"Wouldn't you like to take a little drive?" I said, after a bit.

I didn't want her to be in the house thinking about that, this particular day. And, driving, perhaps it would be different. In the house with her, just sitting there, there didn't seem to be anything I could say. Because I knew Katherine had the terrible conviction that Nick would not come back. I didn't feel that way about it, myself, and perhaps that is why I could say nothing to help her.

We took a strange road out into the country. It was a clean December day, with the morning crispness not quite relaxed, but the spruces cozy and personal and warm under their drooping shoulders of snow, and that strange expectancy in the air with the coming dusk so that it seemed you would know it was Christmastime today no matter where you were and if you had no idea of the date at all. But perhaps it was just like any other day. It may only have seemed that way because of the things I remembered.

I knew what Katherine was thinking...of all the times till this one when Nick had been with us, something eager and childlike coming back to him on this day...his good, really good, clear voice humming "Good King Wenceslaus." I knew Katherine was wishing the carols were over.

"I hope you will not think this is running away," she said, the only time she spoke. "If it did any good to...."

"Of course not," I said.

"I don't want to spoil anything for you...."

"Please don't think that," I said.

"I don't feel a great deal of Christmas spirit this year myself."

"I know you don't," she said quickly. "I didn't mean that, either, but...."

I knew what she meant. I knew she meant, *but you don't feel that Nick is not coming back.*

I didn't, and that's why it was so hard to talk to Katherine that day. I knew it would be cruel to reason with her, for I knew that to force her to admit her fear, even to me, would make her feel guilty somehow, as if she were an ally in it.

I suppose it was selfishness that made me pick up the old man walking along the road with the axe, because obviously he was not going far. He was walking slowly, as if there was a weariness in him, but I am not always so thoughtful about such things. I guess I wanted a third person to talk to...desperately.

He looked surprised when I stopped for him as if he had not noticed us coming, and for a minute he seemed reluctant to ride. He did not smile as he stepped into the car. I was somehow startled at his face, because from his back I had expected to see the face of a very old man.

"Nice this afternoon, isn't it?" Kate said pleasantly.

"Yes, it is," he said politely, but with a little surprise almost, as if the weather was a subject strange to him.

"Going far?" I inquired.

"No," he said. "Just up here a bit. I'll tell you. I was just going for the Christmas tree."

Katherine sat around straight in the seat again, facing the road.

"Have you got *your* tree yet?" he said.

"No," I said, "we haven't."

There was an awkward pause, and I switched on the radio. An announcer was speaking.

"It has just been disclosed." he said, "that Canadian troops are spearheading the advance of the Eighth Army in Italy."

I felt the helplessness again, but I couldn't very well shut off the radio, immediately. The old man seemed to be listening intently.

"Which way is Italy?" he said suddenly.

"Why, sort of south…yes, southeast," I said.

"That way, wouldn't it be?" he said, pointing.

"Yes," I said, "somewhere there, I suppose."

I noticed that he did not seem to hear me. He looked in that direction a long time, without speaking.

"It's warm in Italy," he said, almost to himself.

"Yes, it's always warm there." I was wishing he would change the subject.

"About how far?" he said. "I know it's a long ways."

"Fifteen hundred…two thousand…miles. I'm afraid I don't really know."

"It *seems* like a long way," Kate broke in, and her voice was tense, as if she could be silent no longer, "when you have a son. At least we think he's there. We haven't heard from him."

"You people have a son there?" the man said. He leaned almost eagerly. Then he hesitated. He did not seem to know he should go on or not.

"I have a son there too," he added.

"Then you understand," Kate said in a softer voice. "But you've heard from him," she added almost jealously. "At least you know where he is."

"Yes," the old man said, "we…heard…from him yesterday morning."

"How…."

I'm sure it was *How nice!* that Kate started to say, but something caught her before it was quite out. Something in the man's voice seemed to strike us both at the same moment. We glanced at each other.

"Oh," Kate said gently. "I'm sorry. I…I'm so sorry."

The man did not reply. I hope he understood why for the moment neither of us could find anything more than that to say. And I think he did. Because all of the awkwardness and something of the age left his face almost at once. There was no sound for a little but the soft sound of the car wheels on the snow.

"But you're going to have a tree just the same?" I said at last. It was a stupid remark, from all angles, but it slipped out before I could help it. He did not misunderstand me, thank heaven.

"Yes," he said. "We always *had* a Christmas tree. David always liked a tree. We thought we ought to have one, just the same. Do you think…?"

"I think…" Kate said softly, she seemed to be having a little trouble with her voice, "I think that it's…splendid…for you to have a tree just the same."

We drove on a little after we had let the old man out, and turned. There was not much talk between us. I knew we were both wishing there was something better we could have said to him.

But we were to have another chance. When we came back to the spot where we had left him, he was at the roadside again, holding a fir tree by the butt. He put up his hand for us to stop.

"Look," he said, "you folks haven't got a tree yet. I thought maybe if this was the kind of tree you liked…."

I glanced at Kate. But for the first time her face looked eager, and like itself again.

"Oh thank you!" she said. She looked at the tree.

"Dick," she added slowly, "I think that's the *finest* tree we ever had."

"But your own…" I said. "We'll wait till you get your own tree, and you can go back with us."

"No," he said, "thanks. It may take a little while."

"But we don't mind."

"No," he said, "thanks."

I put the car in gear. "Merry Christmas!" the old man said. He was smiling.

"Thank you," Kate said. She put her hand out to him, suddenly. "I wish there was something we could…."

"That's all right," he said slowly. "You have a son there. Maybe they knew each other. Maybe they…helped each other."

I don't know why, but the remark I had made about "Christmas spirit this year" flashed through my mind.

"Maybe they did," Kate said eagerly. "Oh I *hope* they did."

And I saw that there were tears in her eyes, the first tears since Nick had gone away. I knew it was all right with her now.

As we drove on, through the rear mirror I could watch the old man, and suddenly I knew why he had wanted to stay behind a little while. He was standing there, perfectly still, looking a long steady look towards the southeast.

It was a different kind of stillness between Katherine and me on the way back…not the loud kind at all. But I think we both felt a little guilty and ashamed. I think I felt guiltier than Kate, because I had felt all along that Nick was coming back.

Aunt Cyrilla's Christmas Basket

L. M. MONTGOMERY

The esteemed author of Anne of Green Gables *introduces us to a group of train travellers at Christmastime attempting to reach their cherished destination in a raging snowstorm. The simple pleasures of human kindness, as well as Aunt Cyrilla's resourcefulness, make this unique situation one of the most memorable Christmases ever.*

When Lucy Rose met Aunt Cyrilla coming downstairs, somewhat flushed and breathless from her ascent to the garret, with a big, flat-covered basket hanging over her plump arm, she gave a little sigh of despair. Lucy Rose had done her brave best for some years—in fact, ever since she had put up her hair and lengthened her skirts—to break Aunt Cyrilla of the habit of carrying that basket with her every time she went to Pembroke; but Aunt Cyrilla still insisted on taking it and only laughed at what she called Lucy Rose's "finicky notions."

Lucy Rose had a horrible, haunting idea that it was extremely provincial for her aunt always to take the big basket, packed full of country good things, whenever she went to visit Edward and Geraldine. Geraldine was so stylish, and might think it queer; and then Aunt Cyrilla always would carry it on her arm and give cookies and apples and molasses taffy out of it to every child she encountered and, just as often as not, to older folks too.

Lucy Rose, when she went to town with Aunt Cyrilla, felt chagrined over this—all of which goes to prove that Lucy was as yet very young and had a great deal to learn in this world. That troublesome worry over what Geraldine would think nerved her to make a protest in this instance.

"Now, Aunt C'rilla," she pleaded, "you're surely not going to take that funny old basket to Pembroke this time—Christmas Day and all."

"'Deed and 'deed I am," returned Aunt Cyrilla briskly, as she put it on the table and proceeded to dust it out.

"I never went to see Edward and Geraldine since they were married that I didn't take a basket of good things along with me for them, and I'm not going to stop now. As for it's being Christmas, all the more reason. Edward is always real glad to get some of the old farmhouse goodies. He says they beat city cooking all hollow, and so they do."

"But it's so countrified," moaned Lucy Rose.

"Well, I am countrified," said Aunt Cyrilla firmly, "and so are you. And what's more, I don't see that it's anything to be ashamed of. You've got some real silly pride about you, Lucy Rose. You'll grow out of it in time, but just now it is giving you a lot of trouble."

"The basket is a lot of trouble," said Lucy Rose crossly.

"You're always mislaying it or afraid you will. And it does look so funny to be walking through the streets with that big, bulgy basket hanging on your arm."

"I'm not a mite worried about its looks," returned Aunt Cyrilla calmly.

"As for its being a trouble, why, maybe it is, but I have that, and other people have the pleasure of it. Edward and Geraldine don't need it—I know that—but there may be those that will. And if it hurts your feelings to walk 'longside of a countrified old lady with a countrified basket, why, you can just fall behind, as it were."

Aunt Cyrilla nodded and smiled good-humouredly, and Lucy Rose, though she privately held to her own opinion, had to smile too.

"Now, let me see," said Aunt Cyrilla reflectively, tapping the snowy kitchen table with the point of her plump, dimpled forefinger, "what shall I take? That big fruitcake for one thing—Edward does like my fruitcake; and that cold boiled tongue for another. Those three mince pies too, they'd spoil before we got back or your uncle'd make himself sick eating them—mince pie is his besetting sin. And that little stone bottle full of cream—Geraldine may carry any amount of style, but I've yet to see her look down on real good country cream, Lucy Rose; and another bottle of my raspberry vinegar. That plate of jelly cookies and doughnuts will please the children and fill up the chinks, and you can bring me that box of ice cream candy out of the pantry, and that bag of striped candy sticks your uncle brought home from the corner last night. And apples, of course—three or four dozen of those good eaters—and a little pot of my greengage preserves—Edward'll like that. And some sandwiches and pound cake for a snack for ourselves. Now, I guess that will do for eatables. The presents for the children can go in on top. There's a doll for Daisy and the little boat your uncle made Ray and a tatted lace handkerchief apiece for the twins, and the crochet hood for the baby. Now, is that all?"

"There's a cold roast chicken in the pantry," said Lucy Rose wickedly, "and the pig Uncle Leo is hanging up in the porch. Couldn't you put them in too?"

Aunt Cyrilla smiled broadly. "Well, I guess we'll leave the pig alone; but since you have reminded me of it, the chicken may as well go in. I can make room."

Lucy Rose, in spite of her prejudices, helped with the packing and, not having been trained under Aunt Cyrilla's eye for nothing, did it very well too, with much clever economy of space. But when Aunt Cyrilla had put in as a finishing touch a big bouquet of pink and white everlastings and tied the bulging covers down with a firm hand, Lucy Rose stood over the basket and whispered vindictively: "Some day I'm going to burn this basket—when I get courage enough. Then there'll be an end of lugging it everywhere we go like a—like an old market-woman."

Uncle Leopold came in just then, shaking his head dubiously. He was not going to spend Christmas with Edward and Geraldine, and perhaps the prospect of having to cook and eat his Christmas dinner all alone made him pessimistic.

"I mistrust you folks won't get to Pembroke tomorrow," he said sagely. "It's going to storm."

Aunt Cyrilla did not worry over this. She believed matters of this kind were pre-ordained, and she slept calmly. But Lucy Rose got up three times in the night to see if it were storming, and when she did sleep had horrible nightmares of struggling through blinding snowstorms dragging Aunt Cyrilla's Christmas basket along with her. It was not snowing in the early morning, and Uncle Leopold drove Aunt Cyrilla and Lucy Rose and the basket to the station, four miles off. When they reached there the air was thick with flying flakes. The stationmaster sold them their tickets with a grim face.

"If there's any more snow comes, the trains might as well keep Christmas too," he said.

"There's been so much snow already that traffic is blocked half the time, and now there ain't no place to shovel the snow off onto."

Aunt Cyrilla said that if the train were to get to Pembroke in time for Christmas, it would get there; and she opened her basket and gave the stationmaster and three small boys an apple apiece.

"That's the beginning," groaned Lucy Rose to herself.

When their train came along Aunt Cyrilla established herself in one seat and her basket in another, and looked beamingly around her at her fellow travellers. These were few in number—a delicate little woman at the end of the car, with a baby and four other children, a young girl across the aisle with a pale, pretty face, a sunburned lad three seats ahead in a khaki uniform, a very handsome, imposing old lady in a sealskin coat ahead of him, and a thin young man with spectacles opposite.

"A minister," reflected Aunt Cyrilla, beginning to classify, "who takes better care of other folks' souls than of his own body; and that woman in the sealskin is discontented and cross at something—got up too early to catch the train, maybe; and that young chap must be one of the boys not long out of the hospital. That woman's children look as if they haven't enjoyed a square meal since they were born; and if that girl across from me has a mother, I'd like to know what the woman means, letting her daughter go from home in this weather in clothes like that."

Lucy Rose merely wondered uncomfortably what the others thought of Aunt Cyrilla's basket. They expected to reach Pembroke that night, but as the day wore on the storm grew worse. Twice the train had to stop while the train hands dug it out. The third time it could not go on. It was dusk when the conductor came through the train, replying brusquely to the questions of the anxious passengers.

"A nice lookout for Christmas—no, impossible to go on or back—track blocked for miles—what's that madam?—no, no station near—woods for miles. We're here for the night. These storms of late have played the mischief with everything."

"Oh, dear," groaned Lucy Rose.

Aunt Cyrilla looked at her basket complacently. "At any rate, we won't starve," she said.

The pale, pretty girl seemed indifferent. The sealskin lady looked crosser than ever. The khaki boy said, "Just my luck," and two of the children began to cry. Aunt Cyrilla took some apples and striped candy sticks from her basket and carried them to them. She lifted the oldest into her ample lap and soon had them all around her, laughing and contented. The rest of the travellers straggled over to the corner and drifted into conversation. The khaki boy said it was hard times not to get home for Christmas, after all.

"I was invalided from South Africa three months ago, and I've been in the hospital at Netley ever since. Reached Halifax three days ago and telegraphed the old folks I'd eat my Christmas dinner with them, and to have an extra-big turkey because I didn't have any last year. They'll be badly disappointed."

He looked disappointed too. One khaki sleeve hung empty by his side. Aunt Cyrilla passed him an apple.

"We were all going down to Grandpa's for Christmas," said the little mother's oldest boy dolefully.

"We've never been there before, and it's just too bad."

He looked as if he wanted to cry, but thought better of it and bit off a mouthful of candy.

"Will there be any Santa Clause on the train?" demanded his small sister tearfully. "Jack says there won't."

"I guess he'll find you out," said Aunt Cyrilla reassuringly.

The pale pretty girl came up and took the baby from the tired mother. "What a dear little fellow," she said softly.

"Are you going home for Christmas too?" asked Aunt Cyrilla.

The girl shook her head. "I haven't any home. I'm just a shop girl out of work at present, and I'm going to Pembroke to look for some."

Aunt Cyrilla went to her basket and took out a cream candy. "I guess we might as well enjoy ourselves. Let's eat it all up and have a good time. Maybe we'll get down to Pembroke in the morning."

The little group grew cheerful as they nibbled and even the pale girl brightened up. The little mother told Aunt Cyrilla her story aside. She had been long estranged from her family, who had disapproved of her marriage. Her husband had died the previous summer, leaving her in poor circumstances.

"Father wrote to me last week and asked me to let bygones be bygones and come home for Christmas. I was so glad. And the children's hearts were set on it. It seems too bad that we are not to there. I have to be back at work the morning after Christmas."

The khaki boy came up again and shared the candy. He told amusing stories of campaigning in South Africa. The minister came too, and listened, and even the sealskin lady turned her head over her shoulder.

By and by the children fell asleep, one on Aunt Cyrilla's lap and one on Lucy Rose's, and two on the seat. Aunt Cyrilla and the pale girl helped the mother make up beds for them. The minister gave his overcoat and the sealskin lady came forward with a shawl.

"This will do for the baby," she said.

"We must get up some Santa Claus for these youngsters," said the khaki boy. "Let's hang their stockings on the wall and fill 'em up as best we can. I've nothing about me but some hard cash and a jack-knife. I'll give each of 'em a quarter and the boy can have the knife."

"I've nothing but money either," said the sealskin lady regretfully.

Aunt Cyrilla glanced at the little mother. She had fallen asleep with her head against the seat-back.

"I've got a basket over there," said Aunt Cyrilla firmly, "and I've some presents in it that I was taking to my nephew's children. I'm going to give 'em to these. As for the money, I think the mother is the one for it to go to. She's been telling me her story, and a pitiful one it is. Let's make up a little purse among us for a Christmas present."

The idea met with favour. The khaki boy passed his cap and everybody contributed. The sealskin lady put in a crumpled note. When Aunt Cyrilla straightened it out she saw that it was for twenty dollars. Meanwhile, Lucy Rose had brought the basket. She smiled at Aunt Cyrilla as she lugged it down the aisle and Aunt Cyrilla smiled back. Lucy Rose had never touched that basket of her own accord before.

Ray's boat went to Jacky, and Daisy's doll to his oldest sister, the twins' lace handkerchiefs to the two smaller girls, and the hood to the baby. Then the stockings were filled up with doughnuts and jelly cookies and the money was put in an envelope and pinned to the little mother's jacket.

"That baby is such a dear little fellow," said the sealskin lady gently.

"He looks something like my little son. He died eighteen Christmases ago."

Aunt Cyrilla put her hand over the lady's kid glove. "So did mine," she said.

Then the two women smiled tenderly at each other. Afterwards they rested from their labours and all had what Aunt Cyrilla called a "snack" of sandwiches and pound cake. The khaki boy said he hadn't tasted anything half so good since he left home.

"They didn't give us pound cake in South Africa," he said.

When morning came the storm was still raging. The children wakened and went wild with delight over their stockings. The little mother found her envelope and tried to utter thanks and broke down; and nobody knew what to say or do, when the conductor fortunately came in and made a diversion telling them they might as well resign themselves to spending Christmas on the train.

"This is serious," said the khaki boy, "when you consider that we've no provisions. Don't mind for myself, used to half rations or no rations at all. But these kiddies will have tremendous appetites."

Then Aunt Cyrilla rose to the occasion.

"I've got some emergency rations here," she announced.

"There's plenty for all and we'll have our Christmas dinner, although a cold one. Breakfast first thing. There's a sandwich apiece left and we must fill up on what is left of the cookies and doughnuts and save the rest for a real good spread at dinnertime. The only thing is, I haven't any bread."

"I've a box of soda crackers," said the little mother eagerly.

Nobody in that car will ever forget that Christmas. To begin with, after breakfast they had a concert. The khaki boy gave two recitations, sang three songs, and gave a whistling solo. Lucy Rose gave three recitations and the minister a comic reading. The pale shop girl sang two songs.

It was agreed that the khaki boy's whistling solo was the best number, and Aunt Cyrilla gave him the bouquet of everlastings as a reward of merit. Then the conductor came in with the cheerful news that the storm was almost over and he thought the track would be cleared in a few hours.

"If we can get to the next station we'll be all right." he said. "The branch joins the main line there and the tracks will be clear."

At noon they had dinner. The train hands were invited in to share it. The minister carved the chicken with the brakeman's jackknife and the Khaki boy cut up the tongue and the mince pies while the sealskin lady mixed the raspberry vinegar with its due proportion of water. Bits of paper served as plates. The train furnished a couple of glasses, a tin pint cup was discovered and given to the children, Aunt Cyrilla and Lucy Rose and the sealskin lady drank, turnabout, from the latter's graduated medicine glass, the shop girl and the little mother shared one of the empty bottles, and the khaki boy, the minister, and the train men drank out of the other bottle.

Everybody declared they had never enjoyed a meal more in their lives. Certainly it was a merry one, and Aunt Cyrilla's cooking was never more appreciated; indeed, the bones of the chicken and the pot of preserves were all that was left. They could not eat the preserves because they had no spoons, so Aunt Cyrilla gave them to the little mother.

When all was over, a hearty vote of thanks was passed to Aunt Cyrilla and her basket. The sealskin lady wanted to know how she made her pound cake, and the khaki boy asked for her recipe for jelly cookies. And when two hours later the conductor came in and said the snowploughs had got along and they'd soon be starting, they all wonder if it could really be less than twenty-four hours since they met.

"I feel as if I'd been campaigning with you my life," said the khaki boy.

At the next station they all parted. The little mother and the children had to take the next train back home. The minister stayed there, and the khaki boy and sealskin lady changed trains. The sealskin lady shook Aunt Cyrilla's hand. She no longer looked discontented or cross.

"This has been the pleasantest Christmas I have ever spent," she said heartily. "I shall never forget that wonderful basket of ours. The little shop girl is going home with me. I've promised her a place in my husband's store."

When Aunt Cyrilla and Lucy Rose reached Pembroke there was nobody to meet them because everyone had given up expecting them. It was not far from the station to Edward's house and Aunt Cyrilla elected to walk.

"I'll carry the basket," said Lucy Rose. Aunt Cyrilla relinquished it with a smile. Lucy Rose smiled too.

"It's a blessed old basket," said the latter, "and I love it. Pease forget all the silly things I ever said about it, Aunt C'rilla."

A Call in December

ALDEN NOWLAN

*Alden Nowlan paints a disturbing but realistic picture of a bleak Christmas
many decades ago, when stark poverty in the rural backwoods of the
Maritimes was quite common.*

We stopped at the De La Garde shack. Not even tarpapered,
this one: naked boards the colour of a Canadian winter, the
log sills set on an island of yellowish ice.

"See that ice?" the old man asked disgustedly.

"They built that shack right smack in the middle of a bog hole.
Could have built it anywhere. But they built it in a bog hole. What
you gonna do for that kind of people?"

At the time we were taking them Christmas gifts: twenty-four
pounds of flour, a roast of beef, two packages of margarine. The old
man didn't knock. He walked into the shack and I followed him. I
coughed, meeting the fumes of coal oil and the acrid smoke of green
maple. Coal oil has to be poured on such wood frequently or the fire
will succumb to the moisture and fizzle out.

The girl slumped on the open oven door, clutching a bundle
shrouded in a dirty flannel blanket. Greasy black hair like a tangle

of snarled shoelaces fell to her sloping shoulders. She looked up at us, grinning. Her eyes narrowed suddenly, became foxlike and suspicious. The grin vanished. She bent down quickly, the hair flopping over her face, and kissed the hidden baby.

"Mummy loves you," she crooned. "Mummy won't let nobody take her baby."

The old man laid the margarine on the bed. There were neither pillows, quilts, nor blankets on the bed: a pile of limp, nauseating rags, crumpled undershirts, socks, scarves, slips, shirts, sweaters, an army tunic, gathered together like a nest so that one knew without being told that something alive had slept there.

"Brought you a little somethin' from the Christmas tree in town," the old man said, shuffling in embarrassment but also proud of what he had done and desirous of thanks.

She looked up again.

"Gee. Thanks," she giggled, her eyes soft and remote as a heifer's.

I put the flour and meat on the table, shoving aside plates which had gone unwashed so long that the scraps of food cemented to them had become unrecognizable, ceasing to be bits of beans or shreds of sardine or flecks of mustard and becoming simply dirt, obscene and anonymous.

"Billy's gone to work," she explained. "Ain't nobody here but me and the baby."

She drew the blankets back from the child's face and kissed his forehead fervently. He lay motionless, his eyes flat and unfocused, only his dull white face protruding from the stained pink flannel.

"Mummy loves you, baby. Oh yes, Mummy loves you. Yes. Mummy loves you. Mummy won't let nobody take her baby away. Mummy's gonna keep her little baby forever and ever. Yes Mummy's gonna keep her little baby…ain't nobody gonna take my baby."

Her voice trailed away in a wordless chant. She kissed him again and again, the moisture of her spittle glistening on his cheeks, neck, and forehead, his eyes unreachable.

"Glad to hear Billy's workin'," the old man said. He glanced down at the baby.

"Little feller looks kinda peaked," he said. Her head jerked up, tossing the hair back.

"What you mean?" she shrilled, her voice pregnant with terror and warning like a cornered animal's.

"Didn't mean nothin'," the old man soothed her. "Just said he looks a little peaked, that's all."

"Ain't nobody gonna take my baby."

She turned back to the child and repeated the ritual of kisses, smothering him, moaning.

"Ain't nobody gonna take my baby," she whispered. "Ain't nobody gonna take my little baby away from me."

The old man looked at me and winked and shook his head as if he were listening to a story and was not yet sure whether it was supposed to be sad or funny.

"Ain't nobody gonna take my baby," she whispered.

I looked around the room. The bed. The stove. The table. A chair without a back. Corrugated cardboard nailed to the walls to keep out the wind and prevent the snow from sifting in through the cracks. Three pictures: Jesus Christ, Queen Elizabeth II, Elizabeth Taylor. I winked back at the old man, wanting to laugh and wanting to cry and strangely ashamed that I could not choose between tears and laughter.

"Ain't nobody gonna take my baby," she reiterated with the single-mindedness found in birds, children, and the insane.

"We ain't from the welfare, Rita," the old man said.

She looked up again. "You ain't?"

"No. We just come to bring you this stuff…just a few little things from the Christmas tree in town. Just some stuff to help you out a little bit at Christmas time."

She giggled and hid her head.

"Ain't nobody gonna take my baby."

"Hope not, Rita," the old man said. "Hope not."

I looked down at the floor. Rough boards laid on the ground, the ice visible through the cracks. Pieces of bark. Bits of something that may once have been intended for food. A crust of stale bread. A broken shoelace. Two empty sardine cans, their tops drawn back like the open mouths of crocodiles. Beer bottle caps. Bits of tinfoil and Cellophane.

"Well. Merry Christmas, Rita," the old man said, turning to the door.

"Merry Christmas," I echoed.

"Same to yourself," Rita replied, her voice muffled in the baby's blanket. Once again she was drowning the baby in kisses.

We went outside and shut the door behind us. Rita's voice rose, making certain we could hear. "Ain't nobody gonna take my baby," she crooned.

We edged gingerly across the yellowish ice and climbed back into the station wagon. The old man settled back in his seat and lit his pipe.

"Why in hell does a man have to build his house in a bog hole?" he demanded angrily.

A Christmas Journey on a Still, Magical Night

BEATRICE MACNEIL

*Beatrice MacNeil writes of the simple pleasures of walking to Christmas
mass on a moonlit night in rural Cape Breton.*

The hill before us stretched like an illusion, an embrace, that
caught a fragment of the moon's light and tossed it playfully
over our shadows and took it back again into the navy blue sphere
of the night.

Above our heads, thousands of stars twinkled and dimmed like
the eyes of sleepy children. To our left, the sea yawned and then
seemed to call to order the restless tide. Everywhere there was a
beckoning silence.

Beyond the hill, the graveyard lay under fresh fallen snow like
yards of rumpled quilt, bearing the footprints of night trespassers
onto its delicate sleep.

We were walking at a leisured pace, my three younger brothers
and I, dressed for night, for the pure triumphs of this Christmas Eve
back in the 1950s, on our way to midnight mass.

A light snow began to fall and we stood as if at attention in this white peace, still a half mile from the church, lost in the moment to the tremors and delights of this special evening.

Our church stood in the centre of the village. Its steeple rose and released itself to infinity, while beneath this solace two heavy wooden doors opened up and took in its wings the ripe and bitter-sweet episodes of the Atlantic.

We began walking again, picking up our stride.

In the dead fields we could see solitary lights in the pale windows of the houses, blinking like shy stars. The odour of burning wood crawled through the air and mingled with the aroma of baking meat pies, tucked in the country ovens, awaiting the return of midnight churchgoers.

"How much further to go?" asked the youngest of the boys, Tommy.

My warm hand traced the shape of the candies in my pocket. I was tempted to pass them out, those delicious morsels of hard candy (we called them barley candy), but this was for a feast after church.

We continued our journey in a straight line, myself in the lead, like a strip of wind in the night.

Somewhere off in the distance we could hear the faint sounds of sleigh bells ringing and the warm progression of laughter melting the cool air like breath on a frosty windowpane.

We were nearing the church when we heard it and our voices altogether said: "Listen!"

The tenor lifted his voice in a long and trembling plea that hung in the air like fire on high, then seemed to settle itself again in the arms of "Ave Maria."

And then other voices joined in here in this silence and something seemed to stir the night gently, like the voice of a loved one taking you from sleep.

In the front of the church, crowds gathered like happy shadows mingling on the borders of this Christmas Eve.

Old and young wished each other peace in the warm motion of the hour. From the seams of the church poured the voices of the choir and a sudden hush fell over the crowd.

Their voices and movements ceased. There was nothing in the air that could be called a distraction. Slowly the people filed into the church.

"What are you waiting for?" asked my little brother, tugging at my sleeve.

It was something one could not explain—that embrace, that lingering embrace of the night.

Growing Season

WAYNE CURTIS

One of New Brunswick's most enduring novelists, Wayne Curtis wrote this entrancing story centred on the passage of time, and the powerful attraction of coming home to Maritime Canada at Christmas.

I t is four o'clock on the last day of school before Christmas vacation and my grade twelve class has given me a gift and a card signed with twenty-three names. They wish me a Merry Christmas as they file past, jostle in the doorway, then escape down the corridor to the waiting train of buses. The classroom is suddenly quiet, and I tidy up before making the drive to our farmhouse six miles from Fredericton.

By the time I get home, my daughter, Rebecca, who is nineteen, and my son, Nathan, who is fourteen, will have gathered the limbs of dead apple trees from the old orchard and have made a fire in the fireplace. My wife, Sharon, who has had the day off from her medical practice, will have spent the day baking. The turkey will be out of the freezer thawing.

Tonight we will decorate the tree. I have already decorated the mantel with pine boughs, cards, and strings of cranberries. Sharon says it looks like an exaggerated Dickens hearth. She frowns upon my efforts to create an old-fashioned Victorian spirit in the farmhouse. She says the room with the fireplace is not the "parlour," as I call it, but a practical living room, which should be more comfortable than it is. She does not appreciate the antiques I bring home from auctions, saying they are uncomfortable and old and we should get new furniture. When such differences arise between us, I think I am trying to create something that will exist only in my own mind. I know I am old-fashioned.

Since our university days, the conflicts have increased. Sharon is the most practical person I know. I am full of mystical and spirited ideas for this season and would like to host a tea party, maybe a recital of the children's music or literature classes from school or a sleigh ride from our house using the neighbours' horse, and serve hot apple cider in our old winter kitchen afterwards. But Sharon is the better manager and a realist who keeps the household in balance.

When the children were small, I used to hold recitals on Christmas Eve that consisted of school recitations and songs, and I would attempt to play Grandfather's fiddle. The children and Sharon would square dance. Rebecca now has a boyfriend who spends a lot of time at our house, and when they see me pick up the fiddle they frown in discomfort as Rebecca politely reminds me that my music is not cool. The family makes excuses not to attend the recitals anymore, and if they do it's for my "traditional sake."

With reluctance now, they listen to my readings of Frost and Shakespeare's songs from the plays. I no longer worry about being cool. My wool sweater is ragged, my beard, which is showing strands of grey, is too long, and my necktie is bright and too wide. As time passes, I am less concerned with appearances and dress with a stubborn touch of irony. I can see a part of me in Nathan, who dresses sloppily and spends so much time in his room that is plastered with pictures of rock singers and cluttered with cassettes, CDs, and his drum kit, which he practices on daily.

As I tidy the classroom, I stop to look out the window upon the crowded sidewalk. The students scream and pelt each other with snow as they separate to their flashing-lighted buses. The snowflakes are huge and feathery and with the Christmas decorations along Prospect Street, the scene could be a photograph from the cover of a *Christmas Wish* catalogue. But wish books are for young minds, I think. To the adult these decorations are nothing more than the masking of a cold, raw winter's day.

"Christmas is a time for caring," my father used to say, "a time to look at ourselves, unite with the one's we love."

He has been dead for fifteen years, the last three of which were spent in a hospital's extended-care unit after my mother was no longer able to care for him. But his words live vividly in my mind; I appreciate having my own small family around me even more because of them. Each year his words come back to me and I relive the Christmas I was nineteen and going home after being away for what seemed like a long, long time.

Against my father's wishes I had quit school at sixteen and left my family on our small farm in the northeast of New Brunswick. With my older cousin, Bob Moore, I hitchhiked to Ontario to look for work. My father grieved before I left, but his pleas for me to stay in school were overpowered by Bob's influence. There were jobs in Ontario and money could be made.

The Niagara region was booming in 1962 and we went to work for a paving company in the quarries of Walker Brothers near St. Catharines. We found an apartment in the basement of an Italian home and soon after purchased a 1955 Dodge car.

But like so many Maritimers, we had trouble adapting to the cultural shock. In the industrial world, it seemed no one could completely understand our way of thinking. We jumped from job to job, were kicked out of boarding houses and hotels. We were even barred from the Klondike Hotel in Niagara Falls for fighting. For a good part of that first summer, we slept in the car on the parking lot of the Penn Centre Shopping Mall and used the public washrooms.

I hated the area but couldn't afford to leave. Until a year before I had been interested in books and had planned to attend teacher's college some day. Now it seemed I was without a cause or a dream even though I had money to spend.

Bob encouraged me to grow up, so I tried to break down barriers to a way of life that was alien to me. After all, it seemed we did have the same goals.

"We'll get places of our own, new cars, nice clothes, meet some new women," he would say. Today, Bob still lives in that city with his Ontario-born wife, their two teenaged sons, and a daughter. He owns a radiator service centre on Welland Avenue.

Instead of continuing to battle impenetrable barriers, I found a job on the cargo ships of the Great Lakes, and for a time I had a fixed address. We docked at Port Weller, Thorold, Welland, and Port Colborne on the Welland Canal of the St. Lawrence. The letters I had been writing home religiously with small sums money and assurances that things were fine grew less frequent. So did my letters to Cathy Joe, who was to have joined me when things were better. In Ontario we would be able to get married in her church, a treachery then forbidden by my family.

After several months of travelling, I received a long letter from Cathy Joe saying that she was going to marry a boy from home she had been seeing for awhile. I knew then that I had waited too long and wondered if I were making too many sacrifices for the new dream I was nurturing. I doubted if I would ever find happiness with another girl; I knew I would not completely trust any for a long time, even though there would always be a special place in my heart for Cathy Joe as I remembered her.

My loss inspired me to try harder. I landed a job first with the Interlake Division of Kimberly-Clark as a millworker and ended up on the assembly lines of General Motors of Canada, a secure job with a membership in the United Autoworkers' Union. The money was good. I rented an apartment of my own and purchased a new car. I had a new girlfriend. It seemed I had found the success I was looking for, and my life was falling into place. I had not thought much about home. Neither Bob nor I had returned for nearly four years.

As our Maritime roots grew over, it seemed we were becoming accepted as much as Maritimers could be in Ontario in one generation. We sat with the Ontario-born guys and drank the fifteen-cent draft beer at hotels like the Welland House on Ontario Street, the Henley on the Queen Elizabeth Highway, and the Sun Downer in the Falls. We listened politely to their stories though we were still being referred to as "herrin' chokers."

There was talk of the great hockey players who had played their Junior A days in St. Catharines: Bobby Hull, Phil Esposito, and Stan Makita. All had played for the Black Hawks and the Tepees of the Ontario Hockey Association at Garden City Arena for coach Rudy Pilas. They reminisced about the great rivalries with Hap Emm's Flyers down in the Falls, all of which Bob and I had missed growing up in the East.

There were stories about great golf matches and rubbing elbows with hockey players in the off-season and big car races on the freeways. They talked about the bungalows they would eventually own up on Glen Ridge Avenue and how they all wanted their sons to do well in hockey. For a time it seemed Bob and I had suffered a major handicap by growing up in the Maritimes.

On December 23, 1965, it was mild with no snow in southern Ontario. Bob and I drove to St. David's, a small village at the foot of the Niagara Escarpment to play nine holes of golf. We were the only ones on the course. I think now that we did this not for the golf, but so we could tell our families in New Brunswick when we arrived that yesterday we had played golf. Throughout the game, our conversation was of home and Christmas and we hurried the last holes to get back to the city, pack, and leave. I've since wondered if we were trying to convince ourselves, or our families, that we had made the right moves.

When we drove out of St. Catharines at midday along the Queen Elizabeth Highway, my car radio played songs by Frank Sinatra, the Wee Five, Sunny and Cher, and Herman and the Hermits. From then on I would always associate those singers with that part of Canada.

Our Christmas gifts for our families, purchased at Eaton's and Kresges, weighed down the trunk, but that didn't slow us down. We drove through the afternoon, east on Highway 401. When we reached Cornwall there was snow, which made the spirit of Christmas grow stronger in us. By nightfall we had passed Montreal and had found the old Number 2 Highway East.

The snow along the roadside grew deeper and the night colder as we drove northeast through the tiny whitewashed villages and the open farmlands of Quebec. Save for the odd forgotten porch light, the only life was the occasional yellow rectangle of a farmhouse window, acres from the highway at the end of a snow-drifted country lane. We had hitchhiked this road and could recall those lanes, with their cedar rail fences that seemed to be from a Rob Frost poem.

Now I felt I wanted to visit those houses, even at this hour, perhaps hear the strains of a good country fiddle, played in the style that only the French can play, the hornpipes and jigs appreciated nowhere as much as in Quebec and the Maritimes. I fumbled with the car radio for the down east music. Near Rivière-du-Loup we tuned in to New Brunswick's Don Messer. Bob gave a whoop and we laughed as he pushed down the accelerator to pick up speed. A half-forgotten and smothered Maritime spirit was beginning to erupt.

In the beam of the headlights through drifting snowflakes we glimpsed the half-concealed road sign we had been silently watching for: *Welcome to New Brunswick—The Picture Province.* We gave each other a rueful grin but neither of us spoke for a long time. The taste of my mother's cooking, the smell on my father's clothes as he tramped into the kitchen from the barn, the scent of wood smoke from the chimney all came flooding back to me.

We stopped in Edmundston for fuel; the snowbanks were up to the car windows. Before continuing, we went next door to the RCMP post to phone home. The Mountie on duty was in full uniform, something I had not seen since I left home. The phone lines were busy, and we decided not to waste precious driving time. The French Mountie put on his blue pea jacket with brass buttons, grabbed his fur cap, and walked with us to the car.

The outside thermometer read minus nineteen degrees Fahrenheit. The officer kindly warned us of the slippery conditions ahead, but by now our spirits were well above the highway and we were sailing as if on the wind. Radio Atlantic CFNB, out of Fredericton, played the country Christmas songs by Gene Autry and Hank Snow.

At seven-thirty in the morning, I stopped at the unploughed lane that led to Bob's home. We shook hands and he hobbled down the pathway, his suitcase and box of gifts in hand. I idled the car for the two miles left to our place and my mind raced with a thousand memories.

On the morning I had left, there had been handshakes from Father and hugs from Mother and my little sister Sally as well as a jostling from Joey, the youngest. Grandmother was alive then, and she had cried as she walked me to the highway, her glasses folded in one hand, a ball of Kleenex in the other.

"I'll pray for you every night, my dear William," were the last words I could recall her saying. She died on the fourth of September that same year, a time when I was too broke to come home.

As I approached the old farmstead, I looked at the place with fresh eyes. The snow was deep for so early in the season, and my Father's line fence had only the top strand of wire exposed. The fields that once seemed like huge plains were small and quaint. In the morning stillness, the cluster of buildings that joined the house to surround the dooryard was grey and appeared to be hunched defensively in the snow. The smoke from the chimney rose straight into the sky—the sign of a storm, they used to say. There was a light in the kitchen.

Our lane was also unploughed with only horse and sled tracks. At the front gate, Father had shovelled a place for his car. I parked on the side of the road and walked down the lane, reaching to follow in the horse's long steps. As I passed the barn, I could see the sled sitting with poles under the runners to keep them from freezing into the snow. The woodshed and barn appeared to be huddled like old friends against the winter. I rapped on the front door but there was no answer, so I followed the pathway around to the back, entering through the dark summer kitchen. I rapped again.

Through the door's small window, I could see Father coming forward, peering to see who was there in the darkness. He was also smaller than I remembered, his shoulders more narrow and his hair quite grey. But he wore the same style flannel shirt, wool pants, and laced up gum rubbers. He pulled a knife from the door's casing, kicked a coat that had been thrown at its base, and snapped the door open. Squinting, he bid me a sharp "Come in, sir!"

I stepped into the kitchen and Father looked at me as if he were unsure about who I was. He stroked his stubble beard, blinked, and said, "God bless yer soul, it's not you, Billy, come home, is it?" Then he gave me a handshake that lasted a long time and should have dislocated my shoulder forever. "Look at ya," he said, "little Billy all grown up." He stood back and wiped his eyes with his handkerchief and his big hands trembled. "Ya don't look much like the lad that went away. And dressed right up, too."

He tended the stove as he talked, wiping the smoke from his eyes that drifted from the open cover. It was like the stove couldn't wait a minute longer for another stick, though it was full already and he tossed the wood back into the box.

"Thought I'd come…for Christmas." These words I blurted out awkwardly and took a deep breath as I looked about the room. Father kept his eyes on the stove as if it needed all of his attention. He talked to the stove.

"But how'd ya come, Billy? I mean how'd ya get home here this time a year?"

I avoided his question, noticing that Mother, Sally, and Joey were still in bed, and Father seemed in no hurry to wake them. He poured hot tea and set two plates on the breakfast table, and as he did, we remained silent. My mind raced for something to talk about. Our years apart had left us with no common subject.

I sipped tea and looked around the kitchen. The wallpaper was patched and wrinkled in the comers and the pressed-tin ceiling was smoked brown, in need of paint. The same scrolled wooden clock sat upon the shelf above the sink. In front of the stove, the floor covering was worn black and so thin I could see the cracks in the board floor beneath it.

"The ol' place looks great!" I blurted out. "All trimmed for Christmas."

I felt something between guilt and shame because the place was shabby, because the family had worked so hard for so long and remained poor, because I was driving a new car and had a gold membership and an apartment, much of which I could have done without to send money home. Yet there was contentment here.

"Trimmed, yes. Mary's trimmed everything but the backhouse," he said, and we laughed heartily as if there was no one else in the house.

"How's Mom?"

"She's been miserable all fall with asthma and...oh, she's frail, ya know, but feelin' better lately. I'll get her up just now."

"Yes, call them!"

He ignored my request and talked on. "Well, sir Billy, I had a dandy garden last summer. And, oh, I got me a great shed o' wood up. Boys we had great fishin' too, last fall."

"Did you get a deer?" I asked, not wanting to appear overly eager to see the rest of the family.

"No, I give it up, me eyes s' bad, eh," he said, then climbed halfway up the stairs to shout, "Mary! Sally! Joey! Get to Christ down here quick! There's a stranger here ta see ya!"

I stood in the dinning room. There was a thundering of feet on the stairs and Joey appeared first. He was now a tall youth of fourteen and showed only a faint resemblance to the brother I remembered. I wanted to give him a hug, but he was nearly a grown man so we shook hands. His shirt was too short in the sleeves and he needed haircut, but he gave me the same homely grin. I was thankful that hadn't changed.

Then Sally appeared. She was tall with fine features and long blond hair. Her eyes were bright, which made her scholarly looking. She gave me the long soothing hug I so badly needed. She was now in grade twelve, didn't have a boyfriend. Father teased her about being an old maid soon. She broke away and ran to the bottom the stairs to shout, "MOM! MOM! BILLY'S HOME. BILLY'S HOME!" These words ringing through the house were comforting.

Soon Mother was clutching the banister and hobbling down the stairs, one step at a time. Her shoulders were rounded and her hair was a blue-grey.

"Oh good God, don't tell me it's you! Don't tell me Billy's home!"

Trembling, she wiped her eyes before she gave me a hug. Breathless she sat in the rocking chair beside the stove, clutching her handkerchief. "Thank the Lord, my prayers have been answered." Sally and Joey tried to lighten emotions by poking fun at Mother's faded old housecoat.

Joey stood by the stove and just stared at me. He was holding the house cat in his arms. Sally nervously helped Father prepare breakfast. The parlour was cold when we went in to see the tree, but the house offered a kind of warmth I had not felt in a long time. The tree was open and sparsely decorated. I brought in the box that contained my gifts to the family and placed them one by one under it. Beside the tree, mother had made a mock fireplace, covering orange crates with brick paper.

"The old place looks great," I said again. "All trimmed for Christmas."

"I got the tree," Joey said proudly. "Down there in the swamp." Over breakfast, they brought me up to date on the local news. Father had given up farming and now kept just a garden. His only livestock was the horse. In spite of her asthma, through, Mother had knit socks for the entire family. Joey had quit school and was looking for work. Sally would graduate in June; she wanted to be a teacher.

After breakfast, I went to my old bedroom at the top of the stairs and climbed into bed. My room had the same fixtures, a photo of Jesus on his knees with light beaming onto him through a window, a ceramic clock with its hands missing, a calendar photo of a collie, and on the bureau a stack of my old Western comic books. Jammed in the wood frame of the mirror was a small school photo of Cathy Joe. The bed was as soft as I had remembered, and there was a kind of quietness that was consoling. I drifted into the sleep I so badly needed.

My rest was punctuated by visits to my room from the family. Even neighbours came. Joey came in, sat on the bed, and talked about going to Ontario with me. Sally brought me a glass of hot peppermint and carefully spread another quilt over me. She also wanted to talk. By late afternoon, I gave up, dressed and went down to the kitchen.

In the evening, we hung our stockings on the "fireplace" and Father played his fiddle, sitting on a chair and tapping one foot hard in time with the music. He played tunes I had not heard in years, tunes he had played all through my childhood. He had lost some of his touch, but as he moved his big arthritic fingers, the sound was still soft and mellow. Sally and I swung each other in square dance fashion. He stopped only to mix himself a drink of brandy and hot water before playing "The Fisher's Hornpipe," "The Irish Washer Woman," and "The Ste. Anne's Reel."

Later we dressed for mass. Mother was short of breath, so she stayed in from the night air. We followed the lane to the highway in single file. Father wanted me to drive his car into the village. He and Sally sat in the front beside me, Joey climbed into the back. It was snowing, but there was no wind.

Outside the church, I was re-acquainted with members of the congregation. "Remember this lad?" Father would say. "He surprised us early this mornin'."

Seated in the pew we listened to the organ as familiar faces came in, genuflected, and took their seats. Some turned to nod hello. And then Cathy Joe came in with her husband and two small children… in my church. She had married an able-looking man who wore a parka. Their children were blond-haired and looked like their father. Cathy Joe blushed when she saw me, and my old feelings suddenly resurfaced. My heart thumped as I tried to bury them again like I had done years ago in the Great Lakes of Ontario. Cathy Joe was very pretty, with her hair long over one eye—the way I used to like it.

The organ music grew louder and we stood up to sing. Sally and I shared a hymnal. As we sang, the many spirits in the church seemed to unite, and as the reflections of the Advent candle blinked upon the stained glass windows I could not help feeling I had missed something important along the way.

Looking back now, I believe that Sally was the first of us to follow her true feelings from the start. She teaches school in St. John's and is married to a local steelworker. They have no children. Joey lives in Calgary and works as a labourer for the Weston Oil Company. He lives with a woman from that city whom I have not met. They have a son.

After Father's death in the fall of 1974, our farm was sold to a European group. Much of the money was used to purchase an oxygen unit to relieve mother's asthma and keep her comfortable in a nursing home until her death on May 1, 1982. My share of what was left went to pay my student loans for my teaching degree from the University of New Brunswick. It was there I met Sharon.

The old home as we knew it is no longer visible. The house and buildings have been burned and a log cabin constructed on the house's foundation. The fields have grown up with alder and spruce. Sally, Joey, and I rarely get together now. We have each grown in our own way, in different directions. But like our family ties that stretch across an entire continent, the old home as we knew it still lives within us as life's most valuable possessions do.

One Cold Night

WILL R. BIRD

A spellbinding story of two brothers-in-law snowbound in a cabin at
Christmastime in Lunenburg County.

It was a cold afternoon four days before Christmas when Elrica,
Hiram Preedy's wife, saw him putting on extra socks, his heavy
rubbers, and sheepskin.

"It is a cold day," she said, "to be going far?"

"I am going to the river island," grunted Hiram without looking
at her. "I have heard that Herman Meisner may sell his sawmill in the
spring, and logs I have should be sold before an outsider has come."

"Maybe he hasn't yet made up his mind. Herman could not be
content without his mill."

"One does not always have a choice. Maybe his luck has trapped
him. Prices are low for sawn lumber."

Elrica faced her husband as he rose to leave. "The island is not
all yours, nor could be." She was visibly stirred. "For twenty years
you have not spoke to Simon, and him working his land within sight
of you, and my own sister's husband—all because of the island."

"But," he tried to interrupt, "at the beginning…"

"Don't tell it," she flared. "Some time the river changed and began going around that land, and which half of the river was the first stream, you do not know. Neither does Simon. But you both claim it, like two children. So unreasonable. Stay from it."

"What is mine is mine," he retorted doggedly. "I will go and see the amount of logs that are mine, and tomorrow I will make an offer with Herman for the sawing."

Elrica sighed. "Only trouble will come. Twenty years it has been."

"It is Preedy land, nevertheless, and I go."

"Then," said Elrica, as if it were the most ordinary thing in the world, "you can take this parcel to Elsa. It will only be a step farther and she has phoned that Simon has gone to the woods."

"It will do," he drew on his mittens, "when the children are come."

Their children, like Simon's, were attending high school in the town, and would be spending Christmas at home.

"But that is three days yet, and it is only a few minutes more for you to walk."

"And I am already late getting started. What is it you have to trouble with? We are giving nothing to Simon."

Hiram made no objection to his wife visiting Elsa, her twin sister, but he frowned on any borrowing or lending.

"It is cold or I would go myself," shrugged Elrica.

"Elsa is knitting me a scarf a new way she has learned, and this is yarn for her."

"You two are always knitting," he yielded good-humouredly. "I will take it." He pushed the packet into a pocket of his sheepskin coat.

It would mean extra distance in the cold but he was as much in love with Elrica as when they were first married and could see that, like a woman, she considered such a small matter to be important.

There was no sun and the wind was keen and rising; the snow, frost-ridden, crunched harshly under his tread. He walked briskly, relieved to escape the house without further argument, but all at once he slowed his steps. Maybe this yarn to carry was a ruse. Elrica would phone to Elsa and by the time he reached her Elsa would have some scheme devised for detaining him until it was too late to start for the island.

Abruptly he changed his course. The yarn could wait. He had no time for the errand. He didn't like the feel of the weather. Winter gales from the Lunenburg coast could set in with terrifying suddenness across the sweep of Canaan Valley. He began hurrying, but soon there was snow in the air and the wind was more severe. The icy pellets stung his flesh.

When he reached the island, which angled from the far corner of his farm, he looked back and saw a slow haze dropping out of the sky. Across the river Simon's fields were filled with blurred shadows, but he stared in that direction long enough to detect a track leading from woods to the island. He blew his nose angrily. That fellow, Simon Hebb, had told Elsa he was going to the woods; he had come to the island instead.

For a moment Hiram was undecided. He wished he had taken the yarn to Elsa. He could have warmed himself in her kitchen and eaten some of her sugared doughnuts. Then he would have looked at the sky and hurried home. He should go home anyway, but it would look as if he were afraid of meeting Simon. Anyway the island was as much his as it was Hebb property.

Land rights were next to sacred things in Canaan Valley.

He remembered, when he was first married, going to cut poles on the island. He hadn't felled the first tree before Simon was there, asking him who had given him permission. They had tried to talk calmly, for they were brothers-in-law, but a quarrel had blazed and nothing was decided, though he cut his poles elsewhere.

There was a small shack at the very tip of the island. A mill hand had built it the winter before and had run traplines along both streams. In the spring Hiram had told him not to return. A rusted stove pipe still protruded from the roof and Hiram had tried to enter. But the door was fastened with a heavy padlock so, after shaking it roughly, he went on, and saw Simon's tracks going here and there as if he had been counting the trees on the westward side of the island.

The spruce was better than he had thought. It seemed best in the central part of the island but he did not get far before the light had failed. A shadow of worry crossed his mind as he turned. In less than no time it would be dark.

Hiram faced about. There was no sense in his acting as stupid as Simon. He would come again when the weather was mild, and with his axe would blaze a dividing line the length of the island.

It took him longer than he had thought to get back to the edge of the spruce for the wind was almost a blizzard and he could not pick his way in the murk. Snow drove through the trees in scouring blasts, in thick pulses out of the sky becoming black as a crow's wing. He stumbled into undergrowth and rested only a little but when he emerged it was dark as if a curtain had been thrown around him. An old-time Nova Scotia inshore blizzard had descended on the Valley.

His instinctive alarm as the howling blackness engulfed him caused him to turn and yell a warning. Then he hurried on, groping his way and hating the panic that had made him do such a thing.

The gale was terrific as he left the island, sliding his feet cautiously on the river ice. He moved across and tried to climb the bank but the storm beat him, gasping, to his knees, and he dropped back to the snow-covered river surface. It was, perhaps, no more than half a mile to his buildings, but he knew he could not make the journey. The fine snow blinded him. The fury of the wind made it a blast that caused a man to lose all sense of direction. He started back to the island again.

Reaching it, he moved under the trees but the wind and cold followed him, lashed at him, sent him staggering, searching deeper growth, and he thought of the cabin. He would break in, make a fire, and stay there, warm at least, until morning.

It took him some time to locate the building, so bewildering was the wind, and then the padlock resisted his first efforts. He fumbled about and found sticks but they were brittle with frost and snapped in his hands when he tried to use them as levers. Desperate, he hurled his weight against the door, and the staple holding the lock pulled from place. He tumbled into the shack, pushed the door shut and latched it.

The darkness was absolute and the partial silence was an odd letdown. He stood and listened, then, his fingers stiff with cold, probed his pockets, found a match and lit it.

The place was clammy, chilling. Frost glistened on every nail in the wall, glazed the flooring. There was a stove, a bunk, a bench and table; a fry pan and a kettle for brewing tea, a mug and plate and spoon. On a shelf were two pickle bottles, one containing tea, the other, sugar. Beside them was a jar of Vaseline for chapped hands. Mice had gnawed open a small sack of beans and they were spilled on the floor. There was nothing else.

The match burned to his fingers as he lifted a lid from the stove and saw fuel laid ready for lighting. Outside, the hard snow rattled and pattered against the walls. He searched his pockets patiently for a second match, searched methodically, then with hurry. He felt in his vest pockets, in his breeches. He let a mitten drop to the floor and stepped on it as he probed frantically, searching, refusing to believe.

But he did not have a second match. He gave up when his fingers were so numbed he cold not use them—then had to search for his mitten—and the cold worked into him like porcupine quills. He was so chilled that after a time he did not know whether he were in or out of his body. The thought jarred him into moving. He was becoming drowsy.

He paced back and forth, stamping, hustling, swinging his arms, pounding his body. Finally needle-like currents ran up his legs; he felt queer shocks as his heels hit the floor. He had roused himself in the nick of time.

All at once something thudded against the building. It was a moving object and it came slowly along the wall and to the door before he realized that it must be Simon.

He made no move to open the door but stopped and stood waiting in the darkness.

He heard the padlock bumping about and the door flung inward. Gusts of snow sharp as sand whistled and whined into the shack as Simon entered. Hiram shuffled forward and assisted in closing the door and latching it. He buffeted against Simon as he did so but he did not speak.

"Who is here?" It was Simon all right, so cold his voice quavered. In the darkness Hiram stepped away from him.

"Who is here?" croaked Simon again. "I am freezing."

"Why should you be here?" blurted Hiram, his own voice shaking. "This is not your side of the land."

"I am freezing," repeated Simon. "I am too cold."

"Give me a match, then," said Hiram. "I will light a fire."

"You have no matches?" Simon's voice sounded incredulous.

"I am not a smoker, like you."

Outside the wind snarled in new fury but Simon stood silent. Then he said, "Is it you, Hiram?"

"It is me and I have as much right, and more, than you. This cabin is not yours."

There was no retort, and he added. "Give me one match."

Simon remained quiet and Hiram could not restrain himself.

"We are freezing, man. Are you deaf?"

Simon shifted his weight and Hiram could feel it along the floorboards. Then Simon's voice came, almost querulous. "I am cold, too cold."

"You are so cold you do not understand," shouted Hiram. "I will take matches from you."

He rushed to grapple Simon but ran against the wall instead. He spun around and charged, but fell over the bunk.

"You lunatic!" he sobbed. "We will freeze like two sticks. Because you are stubborn."

Groping swiftly, he ran against Simon, grasped him.

"So. You would get away!" He drove him backward, trying to trip him, to wrestle him to the floor.

It was a weird scuffling. His legs and arms were so stiff that he could accomplish little, but Simon was in no better condition. They pushed and shoved each other without any real strength and with great clumsiness. Finally they slipped on the frost-covered floor and both fell.

"Let me go," mumbled Simon.

"No. I will take your matches first."

Hiram gripped Simon again and the man seemed unable to offer resistance. He rushed him to the wall but they slipped and slid before he could make ready to search Simon's pockets. They swayed about like drunken men, lunging and shoving, with Simon trying to escape. Their bigness was alike. They were both sturdy men, thick-chested stock of Dutch descent, as evenly matched as white-faced Hereford oxen.

"The island was never yours," gasped Hiram, gaining a new grip around Simon.

"Always you are for trouble." He had become aware of stinging nerves in his thighs and body and arms; he was feeling more awake.

Simon, too, seemed more aroused. He struck Hiram but his blows had no weight. Then they fell and overturned the bench. It was a clumsy fall that shook them both.

Hiram was dazed when he rose but when Simon buffeted him he charged like a bull and they crashed against the shelf, ripping it from place. The bottles and jar clattered on the floor.

They were fighting now like primitive men, using any means possible to damage each other. Hiram drove at Simon with his knee doubled, hurling him backwards in the darkness, with one of Hiram's mittens in his grasp. Then Hiram stooped and groped on the floor, searching for something he could use as a weapon.

His fingers touched an object that rolled. It was the Vaseline jar and as he gripped it the lid fell off. Something spilled into his hand. He jerked off his other mitten and felt. Matches! The trapper had kept his matches in the jar!

"Matches! I have matches!"

He heard his voice shouting the words before he realized what he was doing.

Somewhere in the darkness Simon was lurching to his feet but Hiram disregarded him. He forgot their struggling, their enmity, everything. He struck one match and saw the stove.

There was shredded bark inside. He ignited it. The flames leaped and the kindling laid carefully burned with a fierce crackling. He replaced the stove lid and the fire roared. He closed the door tightly to check the draft but the wind drove the fire. The stove began crackling with sudden heat. It was a grand fire, a vigorous, noisy fire, a real warmer.

"Keep your matches," he shouted. Then his lips trembled and his entire body shook but, finally, he controlled himself.

He spraddled beside the stove and Simon came and stood opposite. The fire continued to roar and soon steam was rising from the floorboards. They turned and stood with their backs to the glowing heat, soaking it up.

"Look! Wood!" It was Simon who was excited.

Flickering light from the stove had shown him that beneath the bunk was stowed with split stove-wood. He piled an amount beside the stove, ready for use.

Hiram gave him no heed. He found his mittens and put them on, removed them again and placed them in his pocket. Then he loosened his sheepskin. The heat had thawed him, and now he was aware of his bruises. He stood apart from Simon.

"Don't come here anymore," he warned. "This cabin is on my land. It should be all mine, and perhaps a lawyer will say so yet."

Simon loosened his sheepskin. "A lawyer will know that Hebbs are owners of the west side of the river. It is mine."

"You will not say what is yours."

"Lawyers," said Simon succinctly, "cost money."

"I will pay my lawyer only."

"You will pay a surveyor as well." The cabin was beginning to warm. The walls and roof were dark with melted frost. The top of the stove glowed redly.

Hiram paused to gather his wits for a fitting answer and thought of Elrica. She would be worried, and phoning to Elsa. She was afraid of lawyers. He must be careful.

"The island is small. For two there is nothing. I will pay you fifty dollars for your claim to half."

"The trees only?"

"What else is there?"

"There is the land. You can sell to me instead. I will give you the fifty dollars."

"It is my offer, not yours."

"Then I will not take it."

"You will never get as much again."

"I said I would not take it."

Hiram's muscles tightened. He had intended to raise his offer to sixty dollars but Simon's tone told him it would be useless.

"Never could you think like anybody," he said angrily.

"You are too stubborn to put a dollar in your own pocket."

"Who would you give a bargain? Anybody can think as far as you can. You know you make money or you would not make the offer."

Hiram's pulse quickened. The rasping sarcasm in Simon's tone was too much.

"Elsa has a hard time, with such a one as you."

"You should be sorry for Elrica more." Simon's voice was harsh. "She would be better not to have married."

"She is more happy than Elsa."

"No one could live in your house and be happy."

It was enough. Hiram wrenched off his sheepskin and threw his cap to the floor. An unreasonable rage had gripped him, a desire to beat Simon with his fists, to pound his face until he was unconscious.

"No more will I take from you," he gritted. Simon hurled his sheepskin to the floor.

"You are a fool," came his passionate retort. "Come along. It will be more than talk you will get."

Hiram removed a lid from the stove to let light around the cabin, then doubled his big-boned hands and looked for his enemy. In the dancing fire glow Simon loomed formidable. One side of his face seemed darker than the other and Hiram saw that it flicked redly in the light from the stove. His cheek had been bleeding, torn by contact with the floor or wall as they struggled, and Hiram exulted as he advanced to attack.

"Listen!"

Simon held up his hand though it was obvious that he was reluctant to stay proceedings. He listened at the door.

Then Hiram heard the sound, a faint cry. They stood and stared at each other.

"Who could…" Simon did not finish. He reached for his cap and sheepskin and mittens. As swiftly, Hiram donned his, then replenished the fire and replaced the stove lid.

They kept together, bowed to the storm, going to the riverbank. There had been another cry, very faint, in that direction.

They found a man huddled by the ice where he had fallen. He was too exhausted to speak or help himself and they half-carried him to the cabin.

"Boil the kettle—quick," said Hiram, and Simon used the mug to scoop enough hard snow for melting.

The man was wrapped in plenty of warm clothing. He stared up at them from the bunk where they laid him, unable to speak, as they chafed his hands and undid his heavy overcoat.

The snow-water boiled and Simon gathered enough tea from the floor where it had spilled to make a strong mixture. He filled the mug with the scalding liquid and they held the man so that he could drink.

The stranger sipped steadily and the hot drink revived him. After a second mugful he sat up, shuddering. When he had emptied the mug a third time he tried to thank them.

"That was a close call," he gasped. "Where am I?" Simon looked at Hiram.

"You are on the river island now," said Hiram.

"Island?" The stranger stared at them.

"Where were you going?" asked Simon.

"To see a man. To buy his logs." The stranger shivered violently as if recovering from shock.

They gave him more hot tea and waited calmly for his story, and when he talked Hiram thought he sounded like a city man.

He had hired a rig, he said, at the crossroads, and had been to see Herman Meisner, the man who owned a sawmill. Meisner had tried to persuade him to stop overnight but he had kept on. Then the storm had become so bad that he could not drive the horse, and somewhere the animal had left the road. He had been upset from the pung and the horse had vanished. Since then he had been wandering about, blinded by the storm. He had fallen over the riverbank and while trying to climb up had seen a glimmer of light. Then he had begun shouting.

"I couldn't have called again," he said.

"Whose rig," asked Simon, "did you hire?"

"Chap at the crossroads store."

"So-o-oo," nodded Simon. "That colt I raised and sold to him. Right now it will be at a shed in my barnyard. He would know to get there, and careful, too, with the pung, if the shaft is not broken. You have pulled his head or that horse would not have left the road."

"Pulled him! Me! I didn't…. Well, come of it the brute wouldn't face the storm when we were in an open spot."

"Nor could you," retorted Simon. "You could smother a horse, if you don't keep his nose thawed. If you'd let him have his head he'd have put you into my yard out of the wind."

"Think of that now. Must be a smart horse. After this I drive my car or stay at home. I'm a lumber buyer."

"Lumber! Where are you buying in this settlement?"

The man stood and shook himself. He sipped more tea. He was making a quick recovery.

"I'm looking for logs. Price is going up. I'm, maybe, buying a mill. Hard chap to deal with, that Meisner, but he'll have to sell if he gets no logs, see. And I'm buying the logs around here. That's why I struck out in this storm. I wanted to see the men who own logs before he does." He drank more tea, and smiled thinly. "He has funny ideas, that Meisner. He told me a man—Preedy—had logs on an island. I've called at two or three places where they have logs, and they say they'll sell to me if this Preedy does. He must be an important man. Did you say this is an island?"

"Yes," said Hiram, "and I am Preedy."

"You! Please pardon me, then, if I've said anything out of turn. But what luck that I met you. Will you sell your logs?"

Simon, in the act of putting more wood on the fire, held the stove lid until his mitten scorched, waiting for the answer. It came with dignity.

"There are things to consider."

"Naturally. My name's Keen. L. J. Keen, from the city. Lumber has moved up a trifle and I want to establish out here. I want to own a sawmill, I mean. If you will sell your logs I'm all set." Keen's voice was smooth and confidential but when he stopped speaking the dark cabin seemed an eerie chamber. The fire roused noisily with each gust of wind but between times the quiet was solemn.

Finally Hiram spoke. "It is only half mine."

"The island. Sure, I heard that. But I'll see the other guy and if…"

Simon kicked a stick toward the stove. "I'm the guy," he said shortly.

"Sorry, so sorry," exclaimed Keen. It's the way I talk, that's all. I didn't mean a thing. Now why can't we do business right here. You are?"

"Simon Hebb."

"Glad to know you, Hebb. I've my chequebook here and you want to sell. Am I right?"

The fire crackled but he received no answer. "Maybe you've had other offers?"

"For fifty dollars each," said Simon, with irony in his voice.

"All right. I'll pay you one hundred each, you've been kind to me tonight."

"Two hundred, for the trees." Simon was thinking aloud. "It is money."

"It sure is, but having the logs will make the mill mine."

"You would run the mill?"

"Long as it pays. Will I write your cheques?"

Hiram's mind was in turmoil. Elrica would not like it when she knew he had helped take the mill away from Herman, especially just before Christmas. It would mean, too, a city man, full of talk, an outsider, in Cannan Valley. He said abruptly: "Herman Meisner is a good man."

"Yes," agreed Simon heartily. "That mill was his father's, also his grandfather's."

"So what?" chuckled Keen. "Time marches on, gentlemen.

Now if you'll take the lid off the stove let me have a little light I'll write the cheques."

There was no move toward the stove. Hiram pleased to hear Simon agreeing with him. Maybe, if they planned together, they could be friends again. Simon was not one to give in easily to a stranger's smooth talk and that was the kind they needed in the Valley.

He looked at Simon and spoke meditatively. "We could cut the logs together. There would be no wages to pay and it would be work for Herman's mill."

Simon's voice was so eager that Hiram tingled. "That is what I wanted to say, Hiram. I have a new saw…"

Keen shot up from his seat. "Listen, gentlemen, I'll pay you another twenty…"

They gave him no more heed than if he had not spoken. He shrugged, took a cigarette from his pocket and lighted it.

Hiram did not care about the price at all. He was thinking of how pleased Elrica would be to know that he and Simon were friends again. They had been boys together and soon they would be getting old. He was glad Simon was asking about the yarding.

They discussed every detail of the chopping and logging.

Then Simon lit his pipe from the stove with great satisfaction. Hiram righted the bench and they sat on it, listening to the abating of the wind.

Past midnight the storm had passed. A moon appeared through the clouds. They made ready to leave and Hiram thought of the blood on Simon's face. He washed it clean with warm water and his handkerchief.

It was hard going through new drifts the storm had made, and Keen tired quickly. It became necessary to help him so Hiram went along with them up the slope to Simon's house. Elsa had a light in the window and she was tremulous with anxiety. Yes, the horse was there. She had heard the bells when it entered the yard and, wrapped in a shawl, had released the shivering animal from its pung and let it into the warm stable.

They put Keen to bed and Simon went to remove the harness from the horse and rug it.

Hiram warmed himself by Elsa's stove but he would not eat. He had talked to Elrica on the phone, telling her all was well, and she had asked him to come and eat with her. She had not eaten, but had waited for him. It had seemed an odd thing, their talking over the phone at such an hour, but it had thrilled him to hear her voice.

The storm had caught them, he told her, and he and be Simon had stayed in the cabin. They had talked things over and had decided to cut the island logs in partnership. It had been as simple as that.

Elsa's eyes were brimming when he left the phone. "I am so glad for this," she managed. "Never could Elrica and I be more happy than we will be this Christmas."

Her gladness made him confused but he thought of the parcel in his pocket. "Ah, Elsa, here is the yarn Elrica wished me to bring. See, through the storm I have not forgotten."

"But, yes." Swiftly she undid the wrapping. "I am glad to have the yarn, but it was the matches we needed."

She uncovered a box of matches.

"Such a one, at my age, to use a last match and not know it. It was worse for Simon, all day away with his pipe and no matches. But you were home and he would not go to borrow. So I phoned Elrica and she said she would put them with the yarn on account you might not wish to bring them. So I said to her that matches is something else. In winter no one would refuse them."

Hiram stared at the matches. The package fascinated him, and then made him embarrassed.

He made a great show of turning up the collar of his sheepskin and pulling on his mittens, conscious of Elsa watching him. Ready to go, he had to look at her before leaving, and he tried to smile.

"You are right." His voice was low and hoarse perhaps because it was late and he had been very cold. "No one would refuse matches."

Buying a Watch for Billy's Christmas

KEVIN MAJOR

An engaging story of the trials and tribulations of shopping for that very right gift at Christmas.

We came into town from a place where the best Christmas trees are the green ones you cut yourself. I noticed, on our way into the store, they weren't much taken by the fact that the artificial trees were coloured white and pink, and perfectly shaped. His only impression was probably that it would take him a terribly long time to find a tree in the woods with branches that even.

As their boarder, I had gotten to know these people fairly well. My job with the fishing development office took me to their community three weeks previous. Now, it was the Saturday before Christmas Day, and I had driven the fifty-four miles into town to finish up last-minute shopping. They came with me, together with their young son, for the same reason. They came especially intent on buying an item ordered from the catalogue by mail, but which never arrived. The notice they had received told them it was out of stock.

With ice cream, Billy had been bribed to remain in the car. I followed them into the jewelry store, equally unimpressed by the decorations which, although they shimmered even with the opening of the door, had no smell or age.

Their attention immediately focused on the watch display. Inside the glass counter and behind it on part of one wall, a hundred or more small, opened boxes revealed a selection that could fill the most strong-willed buyer with indecision: bold, simple watches; dainty fashion pieces with brocaded bands; some black, multi-dialled gadgets for which telling the time seemed secondary; even the new, sleek, oval-faced types that showed only digits.

None of these were what they were looking for.

The clerk, a neater, older man who looked like he might have worked there all his life, was attending to another couple at one end of the counter.

"The originals of this watch," he was saying to them, "are today worth about $750. I was reading that just the other day in a magazine." The young couple, leaning tight to one another, appeared to me as if they might be able to afford the original. She was wearing rich tweed trimmed with silver fox fur, he a solid black muskrat coat.

"Hey skipper, do you keep any of those Mickey Mouse watches?" Bill said. I was pleased to see that he felt no reason to be anything but his usual spirited self.

The clerk looked across at us for a second. He obviously didn't think he was deserving of the title "skipper." His job, nevertheless, was to wait on customers. He turned and reached into a bottom drawer. Without a word, he opened a case and placed it before us. I could see for the first time that the one he had been showing the others was also a Mickey Mouse watch.

He left us to examine it and returned to his former position. He continued, "These watches are very fashionable, as you are no doubt aware. In fact we can hardly keep up with the demand. Today already I sold watches like this to two young ladies." I could see the girl he was speaking to fingering the wide vinyl strap and placing it several times across her wrist.

The watch on the counter in front of me provided better opportunity to see just what they were like. The strap, shiny and bright red, was studded with two brass buttons. Inside, held captive, the colourful, legendary mouse stood in a blue suit, cap between his ears, arms and gloved hands pointed straight out, looking chipper and mirthful with one eye closed.

"See, his hands are what tell the time," Flora said.

"Is this the one he wants?"

"That's it. He's been mentioning it every day for weeks."

"Now you're sure?"

She nodded. I knew that to be the truth. Young Billy was certain that this year, when Santa Claus left his house, there would be a watch such as that one lying under the tree. Most other boys were wanting skates, but he didn't, despite the fact that he couldn't as yet tell time.

The clerk left the other people to further debate the merits of the item before them. He came our way.

"Now sir, what have you decided?"

"Have you got any ones with blue straps in that drawer?" Bill asked.

"No, that's the only color, I'm sorry."

"How much is it?"

"Fifteen ninety-five, and that's the best price we can give," he said as if he anticipated that my friend wouldn't be able to afford it.

"OK, we'll take it," Bill told him straight away. His wife placed her purse on the top of the counter.

"Down at the far end…the cashier…" said the clerk, surprised by the suddenness of the decision. His stare followed them all the way to the back of the store.

I walked to the door and waited there for my friends to be finished. The clerk turned back to his remaining customers. They still were not settled on what to do. He urged them to take their time and added how he thought the watch would match her outfit quite nicely. He smiled back at her response.

"Tell me, does it look too big on my wrist? My wrist is very small, isn't it?"

"No, I don't think so. Not at all," the clerk said. "In fact…"

"I don't think I want it. Do I honey? No…I know I just wouldn't feel right wearing it." She hesitated, then put it carefully into its case, closed the lid and handed it to him.

"Perhaps you would be interested in some other style of watch?"

She was now firm in her intentions. "No, I wouldn't really. I have several of those. I wanted something…you know…a bit different. Thanks so much for your time."

They turned away. I held the door open and they thanked me as they started out. Behind them, from the back of the store, came my two friends. Flora, greatly pleased, showed me the wrapped package and dropped it into her purse.

"All ready?" I inquired.

"Yap, let's go," Bill said.

The clerk observed us from the other side of his empty counter. "Now skipper, that's three watches that you've sold to young ladies today," I said to him on my way through the door. I didn't bother to look for a reaction.

Christmas Memories

Sending Christmas Greetings

A CBC Radio Talk,
November 28, 1975

Norman Creighton

*Writer and broadcaster Norman Creighton explores the early years of
sending Christmas cards to friends and relatives in Atlantic Canada.*

B uying the apt Christmas card is always a difficult choice. Shall it be,
"Peace and love and joy abide in your home this Christmastime"?
Or how about "A happy, happy Christmas...A merry, bright New
Year...How sweet the kind old greeting...to every heart and ear."

And the choice today is so ample, among the thousands and
thousands of cards on display! How much simpler it was back in
1843 when an Englishmen, Sir Henry Cole, sent the first Christmas
card. Sir Henry—an energetic and busy reformer had had the
card designed and printed to save time on his own Christmas
letters and also by his interest in furthering the expansion of the
postal system.

It was a card depicting a convivial scene at home: a family group raising glasses of red wine in a toast, with additional little vignettes at each side showing charitable gifts being distributed to the poor. First Christmas card, 1843.

Of course, friends and neighbours had always exchanged good wishes at Christmas and the New Year, principally by word of mouth, even as far back as 1755 when Canada's first post office was opened in Halifax. There were Christmas letters being sent and received and this was relatively easy if you and your friends lived in Halifax. You went down to the post office and posted the letter and lined up at the wicket to see if someone had sent you a Christmas letter.

But if you had friends in Annapolis there was no way of getting a Christmas message to them except for the occasional coastal schooner. It wasn't until 1784 that the first Christmas message got through from Annapolis, carried by James Tattershall who made this mail delivery between Halifax and Annapolis, a round trip of 264 miles, once every fortnight, on foot.

Christmas greetings between Halifax and Pictou had to wait another twenty years until about the year 1804 when Alexander Stewart, the first man to settle Mount Thom, became mail-courier to Halifax. He made the trip on foot with the letters in a pouch sling on his back and carrying a gun—not to protect him from the Indians but to shoot partridge along the way—a bit of early moonlighting, for Alexander Stewart supplemented his pay, which was ten shilling for each trip, by selling the partridge when he got to Halifax.

Christmas greetings between Fredericton and Quebec were first carried by runners, using canoes in summer and snowshoes in winter, or, if the snow was right, toboggans with dogs helping to supply the motion power.

To send a Christmas message to Prince Edward Island was, for many years, quite impossible. The island in winter was completely cut off from the outside world by drifting ice. Then in 1777 Phillips Callbeck, one of the early administers of the island, and the speaker of the House of Assembly, established winter communications between Wood islands, Pictou Island, and Pictou by means of a canoe, a very hazardous crossing that could be used only when the weather proved favourable. But for the next fifty years, this was the way Christmas greetings were sent to and from the island. Then in 1827, a new method was introduced. The "ice boat" operated between Cape Traverse on the island and Cape Tormentine on the New Brunswick coast.

These iceboats were specially constructed with runners on each side of the keel for hauling over the floating ice when this became necessary. Attached to each side of the boat was a leather strap fitted with a kind of harness that the boatmen would don when they hauled the boat up onto floating ice cakes. Doing your share of hauling was one way to reduce your fare. You paid only two dollars a crossing if you helped to haul the boat, but for five dollars you could take your ease and loll off among the mail bags and let the others do the hauling.

However, there were times when things got rough out there on Northumberland Strait. Then the iceboat captain ordered every able-bodied male passenger to man the leather straps, where they stood a good chance of slipping off one of those ice cakes into the frigid Northumberland waters and having to be hauled out.

The main thing then was to keep moving so the legs of your trousers wouldn't freeze at the knees and make it almost impossible to walk. Once the clothes had frozen solid, except at the knees, they acted as insulation against the wind and cold. On almost any one of those winter crossings from the island, men risked their very lives to see that those Christmas greetings got through.

The Magdalen Islands must be given credit for one of the most ingenious ways of sending Christmas greeting. From the earliest times, mail from the Magdalens during the winter months, was sent by means of a barrel set adrift. They would take a small key—say, a brandy keg—remove the head, clean out the inside making sure it was dry. Then fill the keg with mail bound for the mainland. Then the head was replaced, the hoops driven hard down around the chime so the keg was absolutely watertight. Then this barrel was set adrift so the wind and ocean currents would carry it towards the mainland. Within a week of so, it would beach itself on Prince Edward Island, or Cape Breton, or be picked up by some fisherman who saw it bobbing along on the crest of a wave. And once he read what was printed on the side of that barrel—*Magdalen Island Mail*—he lost no time in heading for land and the nearest post office to make sure those Christmas greetings from the Magdalens got there on time.

A Joyous Winter

JOSIE PENNY

Josie Penny recounts her childhood years, when her family struggled to live a happy life against the constant threat of the harsh Labrador environment.

With Daddy working at the radar site, it was crucial for our survival that Sammy do the essential jobs. Sammy was now fourteen and handled the everyday chores of getting wood and water and feeding the dogs. He acquired his own dog team, and Daddy showed him how to make new harnesses, traces, and bridles. Sammy had several new puppies to break in that fall and worked hard with his team. He had to get them ready for hauling wood and water. My brother had become a good hunter and went into the woods daily to check his rabbit snares and to hunt for partridges and porcupines.

When autumn came, Daddy and Sammy got the house ready for winter. They built a shed to store the axe and saws and to keep the wood dry. In the shed they also put the barrels for berries and anything else that had to be protected from the dogs. Everyone worked hard. Mom had her cleaning jobs and her sewing for the mission store across the harbour. Marcie, being the oldest girl, had to do most of the household chores while Mommy was working.

Sarah and I were fairly close, but I was envious of her because she seemed to get along so well with Mommy. Rhoda was weak and sickly and always getting nosebleeds. I felt sorry for her. Winnie was a stunning little girl; quiet, pleasant, and happy. Little brother Ed was spoiled rotten because he'd been born after my parents lost two babies in infancy—Janet at three months and Wilfred at seven months only a year later.

No wonder Eddy was spoiled. Baby Dora was adorable as well. Even though I loved my baby sister, I resented having to walk the floor with her at night when I wanted to go out and play.

The Americans threw so much food away that sometimes Daddy and Sammy let the dogs loose at the dump. It was a cheap and easy way to feed them. When the dogs returned, they flopped down and started cleaning themselves, content with the long run and the food. Many times they came back with their noses full of porcupine quills. Then out came the pliers. The dogs whimpered as the quills were pulled out one by one. That was a cue for Mommy to take down her .22 rifle and go out looking for the porcupine. She rarely came back without it. She'd always been a good hunter. Porcupine stew with duff was one of our favourite meals. The meat was tender and sweet.

On the days the dogs didn't feed at the dump, my after-school job was to stir the huge dog-food boiler on the inside porch stove. It stank, but I didn't mind the odour, because it gave me an opportunity to be alone with my thoughts. I wasn't fighting with my siblings or competing for attention or listening to Mommy ridicule me. Stirring the smelly boiler in the dark with only the light from the flames dancing around the room gave me a sense of peace.

The ponds were freezing over, and soon we could skate on them. Of course, I still didn't have skates. I begged Sammy to let me wear his. They were four sizes too big, but I didn't care. I simply had to go skating.

"Please, Mommy, please can ya buy me some skates?" I pleaded.

"No, Josie, where in de name of God do you tink de money is gonna come from?"

"Dunno, Mommy. Can I do some work fer de store, or help ya clean or sometin?"

I was beside myself and cried and begged for hours, enduring the odd slap across the face with whatever Mommy could grab. I didn't even feel those slaps. I wanted skates that badly. The next week Mommy came home with a new pair of skates just for me. They were boys' skates, but at least they fit. I was overjoyed. My very own skates! I couldn't wait to go down to the pond. After school, a group of us ran across the marsh with our skates over our shoulders.

Several of the girls held hands and skated in circles. The speed caused the girls on the end of the line to break away and fly across the ice. My feet hurt as we limped back across the marsh, our toes numb from the cold. But it was worth the pain. On windy days, just as we did in Roaches Brook, we held our jackets over our heads like sails and let the wind blow us across the pond. After skating, it was heavenly to walk back into our warm house and be greeted with the aromas of supper cooking on the wood stove. My place for meals was on the little bench next to Sammy, who sat opposite Daddy at the other end of the table.

When December arrived, I wanted to go to the Christmas concert at Lockwood. Even though it wasn't very far away, to me it seemed so. I wanted to see it again, to get up on the stage where I had cried when I was supposed to sing "Jack Was Every Inch a Sailor." I wanted to see Hazel and Rhoda Hopkins and little Martha. "Please, Mommy, can I go?" I begged. "No, Jos, ya can't."

"Please, please, Mommy. I'll be good an won't be any trouble. I promise."

"No, yer not goin, an dat's all der's to it."

As she was leaving, I clung to her coattail. She smacked me off. I chased her halfway across the harbour, but she wouldn't let me go. I screamed and cried until I was exhausted, but she was immovable. Finally, broken-hearted, I returned home.

Christmas was approaching, and I was looking forward to getting a few candies and maybe even a toy. That particular year everyone was buzzing about the Americans making a toy drop. I was devastated, though, to hear that the toys were for the youngsters at Lockwood, not for us. But one day while I was at the Company Store, which was the only place to hear anything going on in town, Marcie, Sally, and I heard that the toy drop was going to be on the marsh behind our house.

"Behind our house?" Sally piped up. "I thought t'was only fer mission children."

A neighbour answered Sally kindly, "They decided ta have it fer us too."

"That'll be handy fer us, hey, Marcie!" I said as we ran along the harbour.

We burst into the house and cried all at once, "Mommy, der's gonna be a toy drop!"

"Whass a toy drop?" she asked. We had all the information from the store.

"Ya know, Mom," I said, pointing at the marsh through the back window.

"De air force is gonna drop toys from a plane out der." Mommy shook her head in wonderment.

"My, oh, my, whass they gonna do next atoll?" The little ones got very excited and chorused, "Will I get one?" "What about me?" "Me, too?"

Later, we heard the plane come from behind Black Head Hill. It flew low over the community a few times to let the children know and to give them time to get to the marsh. Youngsters came running from all directions as fast as their little legs could carry them. Then the plane swooped low and dropped several large packages on the ground. We were excited as we gathered at the lodge to receive our gifts from Father Christmas.

"Ho, ho, ho!" he rumbled as he handed a gift out to every child. My mind spun, trying to figure out how he could do it. He must be very, very, very rich, I thought.

When I got back to the house, Mommy was baking delicious-smelling Christmas fare—sweet molasses bread, bakeapple tarts, and red-berry pies. But because it was all for Christmas Day, she wouldn't let us sample anything. She even made molasses candy.

I remember Christmas clearly that year because it was when I found out there was no Santa Claus. I was watching Mommy as she hastily wrapped Christmas gifts one evening after supper. While I watched her, I chattered about Santa.

Finally, Marcie blurted, "Oh, Josie, der's no such a ting as a Santa Claus!"

"What?" I cried. "No such a ting?" I was crushed.

"Mommy and Daddy gotta buy all dis stuff for de little ones, ya know," Marcie continued.

I remember the shock. No Santa? There had to be a Santa! But I didn't make a fuss. I'd learned enough about my family by this time not to make a big deal over things, so I kept my feelings in check. The loss settled in the pit of my stomach like a hard lump.

Even so, Christmas Eve was exciting because I thought I might get something in my stocking on Christmas morning. And I couldn't help but be delighted for the little ones. After some hurried gift-wrapping and romping around the house in nervous anticipation, we hung up our stockings. Then our little house filled up with family and friends. Daddy started playing his accordion. Homebrew was topped up in the tumblers, and the merriment began. I danced and sang, trying to avoid Mommy and the dreaded command for bedtime. But it came as it always did.

"Time ta go ta bed now, maids."

"Ah, Mommy, can we stay up a little longer?"

"No, 'deed you can't. Now, maids, go ta bed or ya'll get nuttin in yer stockin dis night."

I climbed up the ladder and crawled over to the stovepipe hole, listening to the joy and laughter filtering into the loft. Eventually, I got tired enough to crawl into bed and finally drift off to sleep.

Upon waking Christmas morning, I was glad to see the fresh orange and apple in the toe of my stocking. I didn't get a toy, though. Mommy prepared a wonderful dinner: fresh venison with pastry on top and a big hole in the middle. Glorious smells filtered through the house as she made a bakeapple duff, red-berry pudding, bread pudding, and lots of gravy to soak up with our bread. Our tiny kitchen was packed with ten happy faces as homemade tarts, pies, cookies, and candies came from hiding places all over the house. The last pleasure was homemade molasses candy.

It was during the Christmas season that the jannies (mummers) came. They were scary people dressed in weird outfits and masks who danced around the house and acted crazy. The trick was to try to guess who they were and expose them. Being almost eleven, I wasn't as frightened as I'd been when I was small. This time I enjoyed them.

The Eaton's Beauty

DAVID WEALE

In this delightful account, David Weale tells the remarkable story of two almost identical and treasured Christmas gifts that appeared one December in the 1920s to two young island girls. The gifts became enduring symbols of traditional Christmases spent many years ago on Prince Edward Island.

When I walked into the room I noticed her immediately. Dressed in a crimson velvet dress, she was seated regally in a white wicker chair, her long, dark hair falling over her shoulder, front and back. She was beautiful, with large, serene brown eyes and a captivating mile on her smallish mouth. I also noticed that she wasn't wearing any shoes. When my host, who was standing next to me, saw me staring with such apparent interest she asked if I would like to hold her.

"I certainly would," I replied, and walked over and picked her up.

"She's over seventy year old," she informed me—and with that the story began.

When Ella Chappell, née Thompson, of York was a little girl growing up in North River, she and her sister Olive each received from an invalid aunt a Christmas present which was so far beyond their expectations they could scarcely believe their good fortune. Like many other girls at that time they had spent hours poring over the toy section of the Eaton's catalogue.

"It was our prayer book," was how Ella put it. And of all the wonderful items they perused in that catalogue there was none more alluring than "the Eaton's Beauty," a doll attired in a fancy lace-frilled dress with a wide ribbon that ran diagonally across her front. She had moveable joints and eyes with long lashes that opened magically when she was picked up and closed when she was laid down.

But the Eaton's Beauty cost $1.98, an amount equivalent to several day wages in that farming society of the 1920s. Being members of a large family, it was utterly unthinkable that they might ever actually receive such an extravagant present, and so they imagined, but dared not hope; dreamed, but dared not wish.

Another woman from that same generation told me that she always wanted an Eaton's Beauty but never got one. One year, instead of giving her what she wanted, her mother redressed an old doll in new clothes.

"I was not impressed," she added ruefully.

Ella and Olive Thompson were more fortunate, and on that memorable Christmas over seventy year ago, the unthinkable happened. When the wrapping came off the presents there were two dolls, one for each of them.

"My soul, we were excited," exclaimed Ella, "because $1.98 then would be like $200.00 today. At that time, you know eggs were ten cents a dozen, and a yeast cake was four cents."

The two dolls were almost identical. The only difference between them was that one had brown eyes—like Ella—and the other blue—like Olive. It seemed a perfect coincidence.

The little girls named their dolls—both of them—after their Aunt Lizzie, the patroness responsible for their good fortune. Olive got her word in first and named her doll Elizabeth Mary. Ella, with a stroke of childish ingenuity, settled for Mary Elizabeth.

And in talking with Ella I got the clear impression that, in this ritual of naming, the two girls, the two dolls, and their beloved aunt were joined together in a pact of indissoluble affection which has remained, undiminished, over the years.

"I always thought so much of my aunt," added Ella, "that when I gave birth to my only daughter she was called Elizabeth Ann, after Aunt Lizzie."

When the girls were older, and the dolls began to show the wear and tear of being present at so many tea parties, and of having their hair combed so often, their mother placed them in a trunk where they remained for over thirty years. They might have stayed there even longer if it had not been for a trip Ella took to Toronto to visit Olive who had married and moved there years before.

"I saw this sign up on a store, *Doll Hospital*," recalled Ella, "and I thought about those dolls in the trunk. I said to Olive, 'I think we'd better send the dolls up to the hospital and get their eyes fixed, and get new wigs.'"

And that's exactly what they did. The $1.98 dolls each received a $100.00 treatment, which restored them to their original condition.

"I was so excited," said Ella, "I was just in my second childhood when my sister came back from Toronto and brought those dolls."

A few years later Ella was shopping at Norton's in Charlottetown, and spied a small white wicker chair, with a teddy bear seated in it. Immediately she thought of her doll. She asked the clerk if the chair was for sale and was informed that it was. The price was $65.00.

My word, she thought, *I'd hardly pay $65.00 for my own chair, but if it's for the doll then that's all right.*

She took out her purse and paid the money, and now the doll sits in that very chair, in her living room in York, a daily reminder of dear Aunt Lizzie, her sister Olive, and her own Christmas bliss of long ago.

And so I picked up the doll, and was surprised by the amazement I felt when those big brown eyes opened wide. I tilted her back and lifted her up several times, just for the pleasure of it, and caught myself smiling back.

A Five-Dollar Performance

RALPH COSTELLO

In this passage, New Brunswick newspaperman extraordinaire Ralph Costello recalls a Christmas encounter with a hard done by street person and realizes that, but for some good fortune, the tables could have been easily turned.

He was a large man. Heavy set. In his mid-thirties, I guessed. Tall, but not impressive. He had the appearance of someone who had spent a lot of time on the streets. He hadn't shaved in days. His eyes were tired, watery.

It was obvious that he was going to ask me for money. He stopped and waited as I approached.

I, too, stopped. It was Sunday, five days before Christmas.

"Have you got two dollars for a coffee?" he asked. Not politely. Not impolitely. Not aggressively. He might just as well have been inquiring about the time or asking for a street direction.

He was a big man, but there was nothing particularly intimidating about him. He had the appearance and demeanour of a loser.

But he knew this game, and I found myself thinking this was not the first time he had asked a stranger for money. I didn't resent his approach. There was, in fact, nothing to resent. He was another victim of society. There but for the grace....

I stopped as he positioned himself in front of me, all but blocking my way, but doing so rather adroitly and somehow in a non-challenging way, I knew I had more than two dollars in change in my pocket. All I had to do was give him the money and be on my way. I also had some bills, and I remembered there was a five-dollar bill on the outside. Perhaps I would give him five dollars. I put my hand into my pocket.

"If I had three dollars, I could get something to eat."

He had made a score. He knew it.

I rolled that phrase around in my mind. If I had three dollars I could get something to eat. I paused. I had already decided to give him some money, but I didn't want him to think I was an easy mark.

"You asked for two dollars," I said.

"I know, but I haven't eaten...if I had five dollars I could get something to eat."

It was the Christmas season and he was working me over. Why settle for two dollars. He had that. Maybe three. Why not go for five?

"Just a minute," I said, "You asked for two dollars, then three, and now you're up to five."

"Well, I haven't eaten...."

Now he was talking defensively. The slightest suggestion of a whine in his voice.

I felt the Christmas spirit slipping away, oozing out of my body, all but dripping away a drop at a time. Still, two or three dollars or even five didn't make any difference. My hand was still in my pocket, a pocket full of change and more bills than I was going to let him see.

But the game was on and I decided I might as well play it out. "If I stand here for another minute, are you going to try to work this up to ten dollars?" I asked, a bit of a smile on my lips and in my voice. I wasn't go to put him down. Fate, for all I knew, could just as easily have reversed our positions, and I did feel sorry for him.

"I just need something to eat," he said in a voice a bit hesitant. Perhaps he was less sure. Had he blown it?

"It's Sunday," he said, "I've got no place to go."

Sunday. No liquor stores open today. But, no, that was not correct. The liquor stores are open on Sundays these days. There was one only a block away.

"I've been barred from the soup kitchen," he said, "I've got no place to go."

Barred from the soup kitchen? A known drunk? A trouble-maker? A professional panhandler? He had said the wrong thing, and I thought about moving on.

"I haven't eaten," he said, and then his voice trailed off. He'd given it his best shot.

He'd also won the battle. The whole encounter had taken less than two minutes. I found myself smiling as I pulled out five dollars and handed it to him.

"Thanks. Thank you, mister."

I didn't detect any real gratitude in his voice, but that was all right. It was more like the monotone of a tired sales clerk at the end of a bad day. *Thanks. Thank you, mister.*

Then he walked away. I wondered if he would use the money for food or liquor, but I really didn't care. In five days it would be Christmas.

Waiting For Santa

MARK TUNNEY

In this charming story, Mark Tunney ponders the eternal question at Christmas: do you believe in Santa Claus?

It's one of those memories that you are unsure of, not because it didn't take place, but because it happened so long ago and because you were too shocked and ashamed to share it with anyone else. But as much as the rational adult mind may question that it really happened, it remains very real to the boy inside.

I think it was when I was in grade one or two.

We were called out into the hall—four or five at a time—to answer some questions. I didn't know then who the people asking the questions were, but in retrospect they must have been psychologists from the school board. I think they asked a range of questions about our families, our attitudes toward school and our beliefs.

I'm not really sure, because I only remember one question: Do you believe in Santa Claus

I was standing at the back of the line, listening as each of my classmates was interrogated. I couldn't believe their answers. Everyone in front of me said, "No, I don't believe in Santa Claus." I didn't believe them then, and I don't believe now that they actually felt that, but it was as if these weasel-eyed bureaucrats with their sharp, thin smiles had planted a seed of doubt that rippled through the line.

The line kept getting shorter.

By the time it was finally my turn, the next batch of classmates was already pressing up behind me. I don't remember any of the other questions, because all I was thinking about was Santa Claus and how, all of a sudden, it seemed that I was the only one in the world to believe in him. Finally, they asked the question: Do you believe?

Conscious of the line-up behind me, the pressure of fitting in and already indoctrinated into an education culture that rewards what is correct if not necessarily right, I whispered, "No."

They asked me again, and I said it louder.

I remember feeling so confused and ashamed as I walked back to my small desk. I had betrayed Santa Claus, and I had no idea how to make it up to him.

It's funny how you can lose your ability to see Santa Claus, to feel him in the months leading up to Christmas, to hear him on the roof Christmas Eve. Sure, we see him everywhere around this time of year: in malls, on television, as a merchandising tool for every conceivable product. But we see right through him, walk right past him, in a way a child never could.

We talk about the spirit of Santa, the spirit of giving, the real meaning of Christmas, peace on earth. But these too can become words, hollow cants we beat on without ever creating the resonance and magic that once stirred us. Although we continue to celebrate Christmas, eventually Santa stops visiting us.

We accept this as one of the burdens of adulthood. It is not that we don't believe our words, or even that we don't try to live them, it's just that we are stuck in line, and magic doesn't work in line-ups;

credit cards do. When I'm waiting there, sometimes I think back to the child in the line and feel the sense of betrayal creeping over me as I inch towards the desk.

We bring our gifts over such a long journey, over so many years, only to realize when we finally arrive that our destination is a simple one. Nothing but a child.

It had been many; many years since I had seen Santa. And although I have children, I still had not heard him on the roof; although I had seen Rudolph's teeth marks on carrots left out near the fireplace, I had a hard time imagining him in my living room. I will even admit to cursing Santa for bringing the Barbie Van—a flimsy; mind-numbing collection of plastic that should never be assembled after partaking of eggnog and which takes hours more to put together than it can possibly survive in the ghetto of a playroom.

Yet there I was on a plane with my family; flying home on Christmas Eve. The flight was a gift—for my mother felt that this would be my father's final Christmas. She proved to be right.

The pilot's voice came over the p.a. system with breaking news. 'We have a sighting. Santa's sleigh has been located on our radar screens approximately forty degrees to the north. If you look out the windows on your right, you may be able to spot Rudolph's nose."

And sure enough, there was a flashing red light, streaking across the sky. My oldest daughter, then nearly four, had no problems making out the entire sleigh and excitedly tried to describe it to me. The sky was very black, but as I gazed into her eyes, I think I may have seen its reflection—for the first time in a long time.

Earlier this month, my family was at a Christmas party for children at the hospital. Santa arrived, and the kids gathered around, waiting for a chance to sit on his lap and receive a gift.

My youngest daughter noted that one four-year-old girl seemed to get an especially large gift from Santa.

"She must have been really good this year!"

That little girl—whom I remember so vividly because my son had harassed her with kisses at a Christmas party when they were both only two—would not quite make it for Santa's visit this Christmas Eve.

"Yes, Eve," I said. "Santa Claus knows."

Christmas Past: A Victorian Garland

DAVID W. GOSS

New Brunswick writer David Goss traces the origins of many of today's Christmas celebrations in Maritime Canada to the Victorian era and explains that many of our most treasured holiday customs and traditions grew out of the commercial and technological developments of that century.

Though some would give a convincing argument that Christmas has been celebrated in Maritime Canada for almost four hundred years—since the arrival of Champlain and de Monts in 1604—the real development of the festive season and its very Victorian traditions that we refer to today when speaking of an "old-fashioned Christmas" really began to form about a third of the way through the twentieth century.

Certainly there are earlier references to the "Day" itself, which indicates that Christmas was celebrated with vigour in some homes but ignored completely in others, and this would be expected from the varied religious backgrounds of Loyalist settlers who populated the Maritimes following the Revolutionary War in the United States.

It is obvious from reading a letter written from Portland Point at the mouth of the St. John River by settler James Simonds on December 26, 1764, that Christmas was not a happy occasion in that pre-Loyalist era. He was waiting for a long-overdue ship with provisions, and wrote that his men were "in low spirits, having nothing to eat but pork and bread and nothing but water to drink."

By contrast, thirty years later when Lady Jane Hunter, wife of the commander-in-chief of His Majesty's Forces in North America, visited Nova Scotia and New Brunswick, she was able to report that the settlers enjoyed a "gay" season just after Christmas, with everybody "flying about in sleighs in the morning and going to Gregorys and dances in the evenings," explaining Gregorys as "stupid card parties where you are crammed with tea, coffee, cakes, and then in an hour or two, cold turkey, ham, and a profusion of tarts, pies, and sweet meats; punch, wine, port, liqueurs, and all sort of drink."

In 1807 Lady Hunter wrote from Fredericton to a friend in England describing the children's anticipation of the arrival of the gifts of the season. She noted, "Tomorrow is Christmas and the children are saying, 'Oh, Mama, what do you think the fairy will put into our stockings?' Queen Mab is a Dutch fairy that I was never introduced to in England, or Scotland, but she is a great favourite of the little folks in this and the other province, and if they hang up a stocking on Christmas Eve, she always pops something good into it, unless they are very naughty, and then she puts in a birch rod."

In contrast to Lady Hunter's experience was that of George Head, another visitor from Britain, who wrote in great length of his trip through Nova Scotia and New Brunswick in December of 1829, but made no mention at all of Christmas decorations, church services, or the exchange of good wishes at social occasions he attended.

In 1822 Clement Clarke Moore wrote his famed *A Visit from St. Nicholas*. It was strictly an entertainment for his own children in New York, but a copy in Moore's hand in the New Brunswick Museum seems to indicate that his godfather, Reverend Jonathan Odell, may also have had a copy to read to his children in Fredericton as early as 1825. On December 25, 1830, anyone in New Brunswick who had access to the *New Brunswick Courier* could read their children Moore's poem almost as it is known today, and it was such readings that formed the modern image of Santa Claus throughout the Maritimes and elsewhere in Canada and the world.

With the steady influx of new settlers coming to the Maritimes from England, Ireland, and Scotland came a variety of ideas for marking Christmas as it was being done in the old country, where a revival of old-time customs was underway.

When it became known that Charles Dickens would stop in Halifax on his 1842 visit, there was great interest in the occasion. Even though he had not yet published his famous work, *A Christmas Carol*, some of his earlier Christmas readings had begun the work in re-inventing Christmas that the "Carol" all but completed. When Dickens returned to America via Halifax in Canada's Confederation year, there was a plea from both Saint John and Halifax that he should come to present his famed Christmas story, but, Dickens's schedule did not allow for a reading in either city, though both enjoyed dramatic presentations of his works by itinerant readers and travelling dramatic companies.

It was in the early 1860s that the season began to see the first of the commercial overtones that drives it today, and the change was rapid. Merchants had goods to sell and newspapers of the day had space to fill, and the combination proved enough to change the tone of the season forever.

By the 1880s advertising began as soon as All Soul's Day had passed, the buyers often being warned that a shipment of the latest in china, millinery, dress goods, or foodstuffs had arrived by barque from the old country and would likely be the last such items received before Christmas. That such advertisements continued to appear till the last week of January indicates such promotions were not always on the up and up.

One scribe in the *Fredericton Capital* of December 25, 1886, wrote of the change in the level of gift-giving, saying, "Plenty of people give presents because it is expected of them, not because they have a feeling of tenderness toward their fellow mortals."

And another of his kind noted of his task of reviewing in great detail in the news columns the availability of goods in the advertisers' stores, "The scribe is expected to tell all that is for sale, and a little more, to scatter taffy promiscuously upon the hardware establishment, and the vendor of two-cent nicknacks [*sic*], and to lay the blarney on with the skill of a lover."

When it came to a choice for gifts, there was nothing available in London or New York that was not also available in the mercantile concerns in the Maritimes. A writer on a search for a suitable gift in Halifax in 1888 noted after visiting a great many of the leading stores of the city, "One is almost as much in doubt as before...[and] confused by the beauty and multiplicity of goods offered."

To make the job easier, each store had its promotional gimmicks. Many told their story in verse as part of their advertisements. One of them was The London Drug Store on Hollis Street in Halifax, which noted:

Christmas comes but once a year, before it comes you must prepare.

To send cards to friends both far and near.
    And if you'd like to find out where to purchase gifts
handsome and rare,
    A moment lend a willing ear while my friend I whis-
per there!

In the 1880s it also became possible to use illustrations for the first time, but only the more progressive merchants such as Turner and Finlay in Saint John felt it necessary, most still preferring to simply list the goods that they had for sale, and boasting that their prices were "sure to please."

Most stores made some attempt to decorate for the season, though in some it was simply a few sprigs of spruce tucked behind the owner's portrait or credentials certificate. Other shops, though, were lavishly bedecked with greens and went to great lengths to portray community events, like skating on the Lily Lake in Saint John or on the Common in Halifax. Often, the merchant used his goods for sale in effective, though not particularly festive displays, such as a Halifax butcher who placed a "large side of bacon containing a representation of a rooster and a chick just emerging from a shell, and underneath, *Does your mother know you're out?*" to bring customers to his shop.

The introduction of the electric light to cities in the Maritimes in the mid-1880s gave a new opportunity to draw customers, and it was quickly embraced. The Diamond Bookstore in Charlottetown boasted that their customers would no longer have to browse in a dimly lit store, but the electric light made the "nights as bright as day." As an added attraction, owner Theo Chappelle's "exquisite music from his celebrated music box" would be playing for the book seeker.

Many of the stores boasted that they were the headquarters for Santa Claus, but few really had the old gent himself at their disposal. One notable exception was Charles Sampson of Fredericton, who advertised on December 9, 1872, that Santa would arrive at his downtown store on the 22, and would deliver gifts from his sleigh on the principal streets of the city. As well, Santa would be at Sampson's shop on Christmas morning to pass out free presents to area children, a custom he continued for some years.

In Saint John, Santa was not seen in the leading store, M. R. A.'s (Manchester Robertson Allison) till over a decade later. M. R. A.'s was very careful to have Santa depart a couple of days before Christmas, always explaining that he had so much work to do he had "asked to be released from further attendance."

Nonetheless, the appearance of the bearded gentleman had become so regular by the mid-1880s that in 1888 the *Halifax Morning Chronicle* whined, "St Nicholas...was formerly believed in by boys and girls until they were twelve or fifteen. Now, it is a dull child of eight who has not exploded the whole story in the most cold-blooded fashion."

Competing with the merchants for trade were the numerous "bazaars" sponsored by the churches and many benevolent organizations. Most bazaars had a decorated tree as their chief attraction and often their only promotion was a bold title in the newspaper, *XMAS TREE*, with directions to the location. This was enough to get buyers in the door.

Though the first Christmas tree is said to have been seen in Halifax as early as 1816, and records clearly show the decorated tree was part of the social life at the Barracks in Fredericton beginning in the 1860s, and most secular and Sunday school closing from the mid-1880s would feature a tree to be stripped of its treats, it was rare for a decorated tree to be seen in the home until very late in the nineteenth century, and thus it remained a saleable commodity as part of the bazaar scene.

An edited description of a bazaar in Charlottetown at Christmas 1888 is fairly typical of those held everywhere in Maritime Canada at the time. It read:

CHRISTMAS TREE BAZAAR

There was a large attendance at the Christmas Tree and Bazaar in St. Joseph's Convent last evening...those present appeared to thoroughly appreciate the effort.... The trees were well stocked with articles both ornamental and useful, as were the different fancy tables. The tea and refreshment tables, loaded as they were with all the good things imaginable, did a rushing business. Oysters and ice cream were also in abundance. There were, of course, the usual number of lotteries...and during the evening St. Dunstan's College Brass Band played several very nice selections.

The idea that the Christmas dinner should be the finest of the year was certainly well established in the Maritimes well before the Victorian era, and the meal enjoyed then was not much different from what we would call an old-fashioned Christmas dinner today. In 1898 noted New Brunswick historian Clarence Ward put together a description of Christmas in Saint John in 1808 based on interviews he had done with older area residents. In this short excerpt from his essay, he describes a Christmas dinner of the time:

The great event of the day was still before them–the Christmas dinner.... The usual hour for dinner was 4 o'clock. All

being assembled at the table thanks were given for many
mercies and for the beautiful repast before them, and the
Christmas feast began. The viands were all the product
of the country turkey, beef, poultry, game, venison, all the
best of their kind; good humour, mirth, jollity were the
order of the day. After the solids were removed, came on
dessert, pies, puddings, custards, nuts, apples, and other
good things, with port, sherry and Madeira. It was the
day of toasts and drinking wine with each other....

Later in the century it became fashionable for the more affluent to dine out at Christmas. The leading hotels usually prepared elaborate menus and these would be reviewed in the newspaper. There were seldom costs mentioned, and paid advertising was rare. This unique, though rough, poetical presentation from a Fredericton restaurant gives a sample of the range of food one could expect in 1894:

Christmas comes once a year and with it comes good cheer.
  If you for a nice Christmas dinner would enjoy then
for Lindsay's restaurant you had better inquire.
  Just call in and view the bill of fare, All kinds of
delicacies are there.
  For soup, Oyster, Chicken you can get, No place in
town can you get better.
  For entrees, Scrambled eggs and kidney sauté on toast
then you can have your choice of roast.
  The Roast goose and apple sauce will be a treat, turkey
and dressing with cranberry sauce a pleasure to eat.
  Then a piece of mince pie you'd better try I know that
you it will satisfy.

No don't forget the English plum pudding too, with
brandy sauce that will please you.
    Lindsay as a host you'll see will treat you with civility,
so don't forget on him to call.
    A Merry Christmas and Happy New Year he wishes all.

Those in institutions were treated to Christmas dinners as fine as Lindsay served to his restaurant clientele, and usually received a gift of the season to raise their spirits if they were sick, infirm, orphaned, or far from home, such as the seamen who frequented the area in the days of wooden ships. For the most part the charitable treat would be distributed on the 25, not before or after as is common now. For example on December 28, 1887, the *Halifax Morning Chronicle* reported on visits that were made to the Protestant Industrial School, St. Patrick's Home, The Catholic Orphanage, The Protestant Orphan Home, The Blind Asylum, The Sailors' Home, St. Paul's Alms House, and the poor home at Rockhead, which Governor Murray visited, noting, "My only hope is that all the poor people of the city were, or could be, looked after today as my wards were."

Part of each of these and most other acts of charity at the time was a proclamation of the Gospel of Christ and the Christian message of the season. The church was still the chief provider of social service in this era, and since few families did not at some time fall on hard times, most had a faith connection. At Christmas the churches were packed with worshippers. Some churches, particularly the Anglican, were lavishly decorated with greenery and mottos to the extent that they seemed as much like the forest as the forest itself. The Catholic churches usually adorned the altars with tapers and vases of flowers with chrysanthemums being very popular, but used greenery sparingly, instead focusing attention on a simple crib. The Baptists and

Methodists scorned decorations, though late in the century a few started to allow Sunday school halls to be decorated, trees erected, and Santa to visit their scholars with the same sort of treats he brought to children in the other church schools.

On Christmas Day the services would feature more congregational singing than usual and, for the most part, the words, if not the tunes, would be familiar to us today; "O Come All Ye Faithful," "While Shepherds Watched Their Flocks by Night," "Hark the Herald Angels Sing," "It Came Upon a Midnight Clear," "Angels From the Realms of Glory," and "The First Noël," were already popular. Though many musical settings were used for the services the most oft mentioned were Mozart's "Twelfth Mass" and John Bacchus Dykes's eucharist accompaniment. One element all the churches had in common was that the offering on Christmas Day was designated for the poor in keeping with the spirit of the season.

Christmas Day was also the occasion of the presentation of purses of money, sometimes durable goods, or foodstuffs. Most of the gifts were from employee to employer, or worker to boss, such as this example from Saint John: "Superintendent Ellis of the Street Railway smokes a very handsome meerschaum pipe, the gift of the drivers of the road." The opposite was true in Marysville, where in 1883 it was reported that Alex (Boss) Gibson had a turkey delivered to each of the employees of his cotton mill, and that those who sang on Christmas morning in the Marysville church were each presented with a cash gift of twenty-five dollars.

While most of the activity of Christmas Day centred on the home, between church in the morning and the late afternoon meal many folks found time for a bit of winter activity. Sleigh rides were a popular diversion, as was skating, snowshoeing, curling, and toboganing. In Saint John, Lily Lake, just minutes from downtown, would attract vast crowds to try their newly received, locally made "Long Reacher" skates, while in Halifax the downtown Common was the spot to try the "Acme" skate, made in Dartmouth. If Christmas Day was cold and fine, the stablemen could expect a busy day. When the weather didn't co-operate, there was great disappointment.

Grand indoor rinks such as the Victoria, in Saint John, the Arctic in Moncton, and Exhibition in Halifax existed in this era too and where there were no hills for tobogganing, such as in Fredericton and Moncton, toboggan slides were built, and these facilities could expect "liberal patronage," as the papers would say, on Christmas Day.

Indoor games were a popular diversion, too. In the seldom-opened parlours, children would gather to play such games as Simon Says, Blind Man's Buff, Russian Scandal, Puss in the Corner, Blind Postman, Trades, Musical Chairs, to name a few. Many of these are played to this day, but under different names. One that was popular then but has disappeared was a game called Snapdragon.

This excerpt from the Charlottetown *Examiner* of 1885 clearly shows this was a dangerous activity, but the same description could have been taken from almost any paper of the era, which indicates it was enjoyed widely: "First and foremost among the Christmas games is 'Snapdragon.' A quantity of raisins and other fruit is thrown in a large bowl or tub, red spirits or wine cast over these are suddenly ignited. The children standing around are required to pluck the raisins from the flames and they have to do a lot of dexterous snapping not to burn their fingers."

Among adults, charades, singing around the piano, recitations, and readings were popular. The newspapers and periodicals of the day provided lots of seasonal material, with poems and short stories, by local, though usually anonymous, writers who made many references to local history or scenery in the presentation of their Christmas material.

That there was plenty of "liquid refreshment" at both indoor and outdoor events over Christmas is not left to doubt by the era's papers, which seemed to take special delight in pointing out how many cases were brought to the courts on the next working day following both Christmas and New Year's, often comparing statistics with previous years, or nearby cities or towns. Halifax, with its many seamen on the streets, seems to have had a greater problem with public drinking than most areas.

Just after Christmas Day 1886, the *Morning Chronicle* reported at great length on the misadventures of two "grog drinkers" who had spent the day in the tavern and had missed the sailing of their ship, and "leaped into the icy water [of Halifax Harbour] and attempted to overtake their ship by swimming." They were not successful and had to be fished out and dried out. This same paper lamented the fact that the bar rooms and churches were both open on Christmas Day, and one drew as many visitors as the other.

While the individual drinker might mar the enjoyment of the season for the immediate family, and his overindulgence might even disturb a few neighbours, his actions would never bring a widespread halt to holiday celebrations, as was the case when a smallpox scare or epidemic spread across the land. At no time was that more the case than in the November of 1885 on Prince Edward Island, when the Charlottetown *Daily Examiner* noted, "The city was thrown into a fever of excitement," and further that Dr. Jenkins had revealed "several cases of smallpox" in their midst.

Schools were immediately closed, church services were ordered cancelled, travel banned from town to town, strangers turned away from the train stations, ferry traffic across Charlottetown Harbour halted, homes fumigated, and clothing burnt, and the general population urged to get vaccinations, to avoid crowds, and to stay away from areas where the pox was known to have struck.

By December 16, deaths had occurred and many more were on the brink of passing to the other side. Merchants who were anxious to capture some holiday trade received permission to remain open despite the panic. Reid Bros. advertised, "STARVATION PRICES DURING THE SMALLPOX EPIDEMIC," and explained that their clothing line had been fumigated and declared safe by local doctors. In true Christmas tradition, the Charlottetown residents donated linen, papers, preserves, fruit, books, so that those patients quarantined could have some joy in a joyless season.

As the epidemic eased, things got back to normal. The *Herald* noted on December 23, "The weather today appears as though we are going to have good sleighing, which would be very desirable just now as the business of the country is flowing back to its accustomed channels. The large attendance at the market yesterday was an indicator that the confidence of the people is being restored as the smallpox has eased in our midst, we see no reason why business should not at once resume its usual proportions."

"It is hard to write or say anything new about Christmas," said a writer in the Charlottetown *Examiner* on Christmas Eve 1888. "It comes to us year after year," he continued, "bringing with it joy and gladness and often reconciliation to severed friends. Good nature and Christian charity prevail more than at any other season."

It is just as hard today to write anything new, even after the passage of another century, for Christmas today is not, as you have probably surmised by now, much different than it was, and certainly there is much in Christmas today that can be said to be "old-fashioned," even if we don't always realize it.

Feeding the Family

HILDA CHAULK MURRAY

Hilda Chaulk Murray, who lived in the outport village of Elliston in Newfoundland's Trinity Bay in the early twentieth century, recalls the unique and important role that women played in the province's outport communities to celebrate Christmastime in the days before Confederation—particularly in the unique preparation of foods.

Sunday dinner was always the best dinner of the week. Even if there were no "fresh meat" or chicken—and frequently before the days of refrigeration there was none—there would be an extra lot of salt beef and plenty of vegetables: potatoes, parsnips, turnips, cabbages, carrots, and beets. Sometimes in late spring and summer if supplies of most homegrown vegetables had run out, people cooked dry beans and peas that could be bought in the local stores. The "pease" pudding was cooked in a small bag in the pot with the other vegetables.

A pudding always "finished off" the Sunday dinner. This was usually a "boiled pudding" or "figgy" pudding, containing soaked bread, flour, spices, and raisins. Over this pudding most women used "cody" (sauce).

Said Lily Pearce: "My mother used to make it with sugar, butter, water, and vinegar. She'd cook it until it got thick. That was the cody she used to make…. I make cody now, on times. And I make it with milk and sugar, a little water, vanilla, and cornstarch."

Other possibilities were vinegar and sugar mixed on the plate. In early days molasses was frequently used.

Sunday tea was a lighter meal than the dinner at midday, but it was a substantial meal. Most housewives liked to have two courses on Sunday. In winter, salt codfish, watered carefully, (i.e., soaked overnight) and then boiled, was the main course, along with home-made bread. During the summer, a "scrod" was often Sunday night supper. "Scrod" was the name given a cod prepared in a special way. It was sprinkled with a little salt and left overnight. In the morning, it was washed and dried and perhaps hung on the line to cure slightly in the sun. When it was ready for cooking, it was put in a pan in the oven with salt pork over it and cooked in a moderate oven for three-quarters to one hour. It was eaten with bread.

For the second course, people might have custard or jam, or in later years, "jelly" (a gelatine dessert) and "blancmange" (made with cornstarch and milk). Usually too there was raisin bread, and many people tried to have "sweet cake" (layer cake, jam tart, etc.) to provide a finish to the meal along with a cup of tea.

Sunday meals were special all through the year, but the most meals of all were served at Christmas; no matter on which day of the week it fell. The Christmas Eve supper was very much like the Sunday supper: people tried to have "watered fish," (i.e., salt cod), and the sweet treat at this meal was raisin bread.

The Christmas breakfast was nothing very special, particular since children would have little appetite for food. They would have gorged themselves on apples, oranges, grapes, and candy from their Chistmas stockings—goodies rarely seen during the rest of the year, for in the early 1900s and during the Depression days of the '30s, they were luxuries.

In fact once during the '30s my brother Clifford, then three or four years old, found green grapes in his stocking on Christmas morning. He had never seen green grapes before and, at first, refused to eat them saying: "Santa Claus put 'pratie buds' in my stocking."

From 1900 through the 1940s, fresh local meat or pork (your own or someone else's) was the main course on the Christmas dinner table. Turkey has become the main dish only within recent years, after the Second World War and refrigeration. Vegetables and dessert were the same as those for an ordinary Sunday dinner. Perhaps the pudding might contain a few more raisins, and there would be "suet" (fat from a goat or cow) included with the spices, flour, bread, and molasses.

Christmas tea or supper might feature some of the leftovers from dinner for the main course, but for the second course the table was crowded with as many kinds of "sweet cake" as the housewife had in the house. Certainly the "Christmas cake" was always cut at this time. This cutting of the Christmas cake was the high point of the meal in most families.

The Christmas cake in most homes was a rich, dark fruitcake, but there were as many different recipes followed as there were house-wives, and much variation in quality and taste. In fact, some women over the years built up reputations for making delicious Christmas cakes. In grandmother's day, none of the women in Elliston had cookbooks and few followed written recipes.

In the old days they did not have "prepared" fruit, but some managed to get citron and lemon peel for their Christmas cake. This was bought in long strips and it was the job of the young girls to cut it into small pieces.

Said Aunt Hilda, "the flavour seemed nicer then, than now."

They used raisins too, but the big-seeded kind had to have the seeds removed. Currants were in common use, but housewives rarely used nuts in their baking until the 1920s.

In mother's day, cookbooks were becoming more common in the kitchen, and women also tried out recipes given on the "Homemaker's Page" in the *Family Herald*, a weekly farming newspaper found in a great many Elliston homes.

Housewives in the 1930s and '40s, if they could afford it, obtained the same candied fruits as are available today. Cherries, lemon, citron, and orange peels, raisins, seeded and unseeded, currants, dates, and walnuts were widely used. Both in the early 1900s and later, housewives used a variety of spices along with molasses, flour, eggs, and butter. Most women used the artificial lemon or vanilla flavourings, but others used a small drop of wine, or even rum.

Other Christmas delicacies might include a light fruitcake, several plain "layer cakes" with jam between, a light loaf cake with raisins, "patties" (small bun cookies), raisin bread, and "barksail" bread (molasses-flavoured bread with no raisins). Housewives in recent years have added chocolate cakes and a bewildering array of cookies. Even today, most housewives try to have plenty of fancy baked goods on hand for the entire Christmas season.

For many people, especially those with very large families in the old days, and for most families during the Depression, "sweet cake" was a luxury; there was only sufficient at special occasions like Christmas. Most women, unless they were extremely poor, did "Christmas baking" and tried to bake enough goodies to last for the twelve days of Christmas, for anyone might drop in during that period.

In the old days "some people tried to get a slice of Christmas cake from twelve different houses to ensure twelve months of happiness," said Mary Jane Porter.

No visitor could leave the house without a "bit of Christmas"—a sampling of the Christmas cake, plus other lesser kinds, and a drink. The drink might be tea or hot peppermint, or even cold syrup during recent years. Few women took anything stronger, though some would sample the home-brewed wine—blueberry, dogberry, or dandelion. The "homebrew," (i.e., beer), and the "drop" of rum were only served to the male visitors, though both the wine and the beer were very likely brewed by the women.

Dogberry trees (*Pyrus americana*) were found in many house yards, and they also grew wild near the settlement. Anyone could have dogberry wine, and most people did. Winemakers liked to gather berries after the first frost, so as to have the most flavourful wine. Dandelion wine was not so common. This was probably because it had to be made in summer when the dandelions were in full bloom. Women were far too busy with other tasks at that time of the year go wine making.

On New Year's Day the meals, especially the dinner, were almost as good as those served on Christmas Day. But supper on New Year's Day was often taken out of the house, at the "Orangeman's Time."

A Christmas Trip to Town

MICHAEL O. NOWLAN

Michael Nowlan recalls a simpler time in his early childhood, when a straightforward trip to town during the festive season was such a memorable occasion that the joys of Christmas travel remained with him throughout his life.

Christmas in rural New Brunswick used to have an air of mystery and enchantment for a small boy. Recalling those times, I often despair at how television, radio, and other factors have tampered with the imaginations of children. We all had our lists for the jolly old man in red, but we were not shouted at. We were not being constantly told what toys or games we needed to make our Christmas complete. Someone somewhere should have devised a scheme to assure the simplicity of the Christmas feast.

By simplicity, I mean the expectations of gifts, trees, decorations, and food that complemented the Infant's birth, not smothered it. Even though there was a mysticism that a child could not explain and much of it has been lost in time, some memories remain very vivid as each Yuletide rolls around.

Since we had no car on the farm, travel to town, five miles away, was almost a day's effort. What's more, travel to town at Christmas was practically out of the question because the river was seldom frozen hard enough for horse travel and the ferry was not operating. Consequently, we children seldom saw town at Christmastime.

On Christmas Eve, Dad and Mother usually made the annual trek, returning with bright packages, curious brown paper bags, and assorted bundles. As time passed and the road was paved, they made the trip by bus. But those were in the later years when we were grown up.

Their return was heralded by the jangle of sleigh bells late in the afternoon. This would heighten the mystery and raise spirits to a fever pitch that spread, I'm sure, to the attic of the house and the loftiest haymow in the barn. The tree was then brought in and decorated, and at supper we would have the first taste of Christmas cooking.

I remember one year, for some reason unknown to me now, I made the trip to town with Dad.

The morning was bright and frosty. Years ago, there always seemed to be more snow at Christmas than there is today. The runners creaked. The sleigh was laden with gifts for friends and relatives in town. These gifts were roasts of pork or beef, or perhaps a piece of steak. Each was nicely wrapped and appropriately labelled.

I can still see that Christmas shopping at home when my parents selected the gifts. "Who will we give the pork to this year? What about that special cut of steak? Will that be big enough? They have a large family."

Tucked under the seat was a beef hide for Dad to sell. Little did I realize as I listened to the bells and my mind raced with visions of Santa Claus that I would deliver some of those presents when we arrived in town.

There was an early freeze-up that year, so it was quickly across the ice and into town without taking the long detour around by bridge. At the first stop, Dad selected a package from under the sleek bear rug he always used for such occasions and told me to take it to the door. Big, shy, farm kid that I was, I hesitated.

"Go on," he said. "I have others to deliver."

I don't know what made me do it, but I got up the courage to go to that door. I banged loudly. At least, it sounded like a drum to my ears. When the door opened, a young fellow, older than me, stood there. I offered the package, saying Mom and Dad sent it for Christmas. At the same time, I peered around him at the tinsel-decorated hall and caught a glimpse of a beautiful tree.

From deep within, a sharp voice called, "Who is it?"

I was trapped.

Carrying those distinctive smells of Christmas, a lady appeared in the hallway.

"And who are you?"

I stammered a reply, prepared to run to the safety of the sleigh.

"Ah, the...boy. Come in. You must be frozen."

Candy was passed from a bright red dish along with apples and oranges. Doughnuts and various cakes were cooling on the kitchen table. By now, retreat was impossible. All I wanted to do was vanish. Muttering something about Dad, I made a move toward the door.

"Wait a minute. Wait a minute," was the lady's instant reaction.

And to her husband she directed, "Where's that box for the... children?"

He disappeared to return with a great box I could hardly carry. As they opened the door, I rushed out shouting (I had forgotten my shyness): "Merry Christmas!"

Getting to the sleigh, I found Dad had delivered another package and had returned with a box similar to the one I had. We continued in this manner until all our packages were gone except a special one, done up with bright red ribbon.

It was then to the business section of town where we "parked" the horse in the freestand (a sort of open stable for horses) and fed him some hay. Soon we were into the street with that special parcel which Dad carried to a small specialty shop. I fully remembered the place from summer trips to town. The owner was a tall, friendly old lady who was a dear friend of the family. As Dad talked, I explored the store with all its promises of Christmas.

Here was Christmas in a new dimension. Not only this store, but in all the others we visited as Dad obtained the things on the long list he and Mother had compiled the night before.

My small-boy imagination still runs vividly through that Christmas Eve. Street after street, home after home—blazing fires, bright trees, beautiful aromas, bountiful gifts. A boy's eyes saw Christmas in town for the first time. There was something special about it. Something only the power of memory can capture.

It was not only special, but it stirred a meaning of giving and receiving. The pork and beef roasts were the Gifts of the Magi; our horse, a camel; the snow, desert sand. Meanwhile, I fantasized in the gifts of childhood—wonderment, excitement, and innocent devotion to the infant Christ. A child's mind could play many tricks and this was one of them.

Growing up on the farm had its disadvantages, but that Christmas generated an experience with which I have lived many succeeding festive seasons. With all the expectations of Christmas children have today, none could outweigh that trip to town with Dad.

Belsnickles—Vanishing Race

J. Keith Young

A strange old Christmas custom brought over to the New World from Germany centuries ago urges residents from Nova Scotia's South Shore to not let the cherished holiday tradition fade away.

"**S**chiessen oder nicht schiessen!*" was once the strange cry beneath many a window in the town of Lunenburg, which traces its ancestry to a Germanic origin. Christmas and Old Year's Night was looked forward to by that vanishing race—the belsnickles. Possibly this word is somewhat unfamiliar to many, so let us delve into the dark mystery of the once-common belsnickle.

The ancient custom of belsnickling traces itself back to bygone days when, in preChristmas days, men dressed in women's clothes and the hides of animals presented gifts—a custom recalling the Roman feasts of Saturnalia. These feasts developed gradually into mummer or parties of such masqueraders and caused much mischief and merriment, especially with the younger groups.

Because of the animal hides worn and the later connection with St. Nicholas, the custom became known as belsnickling and those taking part as belsnickel—the words being variants of the word *peltznickle*, recorded on the Rhine in Germany.

Belsnickling, although once strong at Christmas, does not stop with the passing of this day but continues until New Year's Eve, still called Old Year's Night by many Lunenburg oldsters. Even yet, small groups of belsnickies can be seen going from door to door dressed in outlandish costumes and usually playing—or trying to play—musical instruments of every type.

Householders are invited to donate to an empty bag carried for the purpose, and it is advised by one who knows—donate! The cry of *"schiessen"* (shoot) and *"nicht schlessen"* (don't shoot) stems from the custom of the belsnickles once carrying guns and it was shoot if no gift was forthcoming when a household was challenged. Of course the guns were discharged into the air, but it wasn't worth taking a chance on some over-happy celebrant with his weapon.

Storekeepers on the Lunenburg streets were fair targets, and all without exception had a donation handy for the belsnickles on their regular arrival after dark. It seems almost like Halloween, except that the majority of belsnickles are older youths and girls intent on a merry time after the youngsters are tucked into their beds.

Basements are ransacked for empty potato or onion bags, and even a pillowcase will serve for the expected handouts. Apples, oranges, nuts, candy, and other goodies are obtained in abundance by every group, large or small, and it is certain that many a stomach groans in agony at the unexpected fare forced upon it after so much turkey and pudding. Certainly this is a custom that should not be allowed to fade into limbo, so come on Lunenburgers: don some old clothes, a mask, mouth organ, and an empty bag; gather a group of friends and tie yourself to the neighbourhood for a good evening of fun—belsnickling!

Uncle Joe Burton's Strange Christmas Box

REVEREND GEORGE J. BOND

*First published in the St. John's Evening Telegram in December 1887,
this historic Christmas tale of tragedy and heroic rescue on the wild,
windswept coast of Newfoundland offers readers a glimpse into the
rugged pioneer character of nineteenth-century outport life.*

It was Christmas Eve, and outside Uncle Joe Burton's cottage,
wild and stormy enough. A strong breeze from the northwest
had been blowing since noon, with frequent showers of snow, and
as the day advanced, the wind had come more from the north and
freshened to a gale. Great gusts ever and anon sent blinding drifts
of snow swirling over the roads, piling them high against the picket
fences, and wreathing quaint, curling masses over the firewood piles
resting against the house. The windows rattled in their casements and
puffs of smoke poured frequently down the chimney, which roared
and groaned like some huge animal in mortal pain.

It was a gloomy scene indeed that Mrs. Burton looked out upon, as
she went to the windows to draw down the blinds. The short evening

was darkening rapidly over the dreary landscape, and the houses of the little fishing village lay half buried under a winding sheet of snow. On the opposite side of the harbour the great cliff loomed frowingly through the flying snowflakes, while against its base the cold, white breakers were dashing with a sullenness that was fast increasing into fury. Seaward, a hazy stretch of white-capped billows chased each other tumultuously shoreward, driven hard by the fierce and still freshening wind. The good woman shuddered as she gazed.

"A terrible night, sure enough," she murmured.

"The good Lord pity any poor fellows in craft on this shore tonight," and then, with a sigh that might be an Amen to her kindly prayer, she drew the red curtains over the noisy windows, and set about getting her husband's supper.

It was a pleasant enough interior. In the huge chimney recess that had been built for open fires, a well-burnished cooking stove sent out its heat, and on its top the teakettle sang a cheery song in perfect harmony with the hubble-bubble of a boiler, its companion, in which a big figgy pudding, rich with galores of suet and citron, was already undergoing the beginning of its long boil for tomorrow's dinner. An appetizing odour came from the oven, where a couple of fine, fat bull birds, part proceeds of a successful day's gunning in punt, a day or two before, were yielding up their juices, as they browned for the good man's supper.

Mats hooked in bright colours and quaint patterns covered the clean floor, and a noisy American clock emphasized the flight of time on a shelf between the two small windows, flanked on the one side by a bright print cut from some illustrated periodical, and on the other by a gay pictorial advertisement for *Taylor's Soluble Cocoa*.

Gleams from the glowing wood inside the stove—bars lit up the rows of crockery on the tidy dresser, and glanced along the barrels of the skipper's guns, suspended on rests across the beams of the ceiling. A big black and white cat, evidently a privileged member of the household, purred contentedly on a settle on one side of the stove, while on the other the skipper himself, with head resting on his hands and elbows on knees, stooped, sound asleep over the fire. An air of homely content and comfort pervaded the whole apartment, with which the expression of Mrs. Burton's face, as she bustled about, and the tone of her voice, as she quietly hummed a hymn, were completely in unison.

In a little while the supper was ready, the teapot filled and set on the stove fender to draw, and the bull birds smoking temptingly on a big blue dish, supported on the one side by an overflowing plate of mealy potatoes and on the other by an equally generous plate of "riz" bread and butter. As Mrs. Burton set the chairs by the table, her husband awoke with a mighty stretch and yawn, and rose to his feet.

"Why, I b'lieve I bin dozin' a bit," he said.

"Dozin'! You've bin fast asleep for an hour or more, I allow," replied his wife, laughing; "an' I don't wonder, after bein' in the woods all day. Draw over now, and take hold. You must want your supper, I'm sure."

As Uncle Joe sits down at his humble board, let us have a good look at him. Short, sturdy, square-set, with a large head set firmly on his broad shoulders; the face wrinkled and weather-beaten, but fresh and ruddy, framed all round with grey whiskers; eyes that twinkled good-humouredly beneath shaggy brows; a tumbling chaos of iron-grey hair above a broad, honest forehead—a typical fisherman in build and appearance.

And Aunt Betsy, as the people called her, was a fitting match for her husband. She, too, was short and square, and sturdy; but the hair beneath the trim cap was still jet black, and the placid brow unwrinkled; and, though the face had lost something of the colour and contour that in youth had made her the belle of the harbour, there was a matronly sweetness about her that more than made up for any loss of youthful charms. Uncle Joe, kindly, shrewd, and blunt, was, by sheer force of personal character, a "leadin' man" in the little settlement, while his wife was known for miles around as the friend and sympathizer, readiest with help of word and deed in all cases of emergency or illness; in her quiet way, a true Lady Bountiful, devoting herself in personal ministration to the sick and the poor. The worthy couple had no children; but this deprivation, while it sometimes brought secret sorrow to the gentle Aunt Betsy's loving heart, made it open none the less warmly to mother the children of others, and many a little one, sick and sorrowful, had been nursed back to health and gladness in her kind embrace.

"My! 'Tis a wild night," said Uncle Joe, pausing with a cup of tea midway to his lips, as a gust of more than usual violence shook the house. "I'm afeard there's craft about, too. I seen three goin' up the bay as I was comin' out o' the woods. People goin' up craft-buildin', I s'pose, though it's very late. I hope there's no one near this shore, anyway; the wind's come right in on it."

"I thought o' the same thing just now," said his wife. "I don't know how 'tis people will leave it so late. 'Tis no weather this for craft to be knockin' about in."

"But, my maid, what can 'em do, if they happens to be out and get caught in it? You know it looked civil enough this mornin', an' I'm sure 'twas as mild as October yesterday; an' I'm afeard, as I say, that some of 'em is not far off. I do hope they got into harbour somewhere afore these snow-dwies got so bad. Wind an' sea is bad enough when you're anywhere near land, but when snow comes with 'em, 'tis awful work."

Little more was said on the subject during the meal, and the conversation branched off to other topics. Two or three hours later, as they were sitting by the fire, Aunt Betsy knitting and Uncle Joe busy putting new soles on a pair of fishing boots, a sudden hurried scuffling in the back porch and a loud rap at the door startled them from the quiet in which they had been working. Then the door was abruptly opened and a half-dozen men appeared in the entry.

"Is Uncle Joe in?" exclaimed the first. "Oh, yes, there he is." "Uncle Joe, there's a craft ashore down here in the Devil's Gulch, and we want you to come and help us to get the poor creatures out of her afore she goes to pieces."

No time was lost in idle questioning, but in the few minutes it took Uncle Joe to get ready, the leader explained how he had come to know of the wreck. Living not far from the ugly chasm known as the Devil's Gulch, he had happened to be returning home a quarter of an hour before from a neighbour's house, had heard, through the storm, the shouts and screams which told him that a craft was close to or on the rocks, and had hurried to the nearest houses for help. In less time than it takes to write it, all was ready; well provided with lanterns and ropes, the party started on their errand of mercy.

"Keep up a good heart, and a good fire, Betsy," was Uncle Joe's parting injunction. "I'll be back as soon as I can, an', maybe, bring some of the poor chaps home with me, please God we can save 'em. Pray for us, maid; we're in God's hands."

It was not more than half a mile to the gulch, and amid the thick, blinding snowstorm, long before they reached it, they could hear the hoarse "rote" of the breakers and the boom of the waves as they were hurled into the chasm.

The Devil's Gulch was appropriately named. It was a ragged rift in the steep cliffs, as if by some titanic force they had been violently torn asunder, leaving a narrow opening of perhaps a hundred feet in width, and two hundred in length, the bottom filled with huge, jagged rocks. Around it the cliffs rose sheer and beetling, except where, at the extreme end, a narrow margin of shingly beach intervened at low tide between the water and the rock.

Into this narrow gulch the waves tore with relentless violence in bad weather, seething and foaming around the sharp rocks with a terrible sound; and far in through this awful chasm had a hapless craft been driven on the night in question, escaping instant destruction on the ragged teeth at the entrance, only to be hurled against the beach at the extremity. Here she lay wedged in the rocks, the waters howling like hungry wolves around her.

But not a sound came from the wreck as Uncle Joe and the rest of the men stood on the ledge immediately over her. Far down below them, a couple of hundred feet at least, they could make out a dim outline of her hull; but no shout or cry for help reached their ears.

Were all dead? Were they too late? Long the men waited, peering down into the darkness, and shouting. But no answering voice came back, nothing but a hollow echo from the opposite cliffs, sounding as if a fiend were mocking them.

"'Tis no use," said one of the men at length.

"They're all gone, poor fellows. We're too late."

"Aye," said another, "I'm afeard we are; and yet I could ha' sworn I heard 'em not two minutes afore we come."

"Heard 'em? To be sure we did!" exclaimed a third. "Maybe they've got ashore somehow."

"Sure you know very well they couldn't do that," answered the first speaker. "'Tis a straight up an' down cliff, an' even if they got on that bit o' beach at the bight, they couldn't stand there a minute without bein' washed off. I think myself we'd best go home. They're all gone, I b'lieve, poor mortals."

All this time Uncle Joe had been creeping cautiously out to the edge of a beetling crag which projected immediately over the wreck; and stretching himself out at full length, lay with head and shoulders over the edge, peering down into the darkness and listening intently to the confused noises below.

"Hark!" he cried, suddenly; and the men were silent—not a sound but the roar of the sea and the cruel hiss of the sleet-laden wind. Anxiously the men listened, every ear strained, every breath hushed.

"It must ha' bin the wind," said one of them, at length.

"Hush!" said Uncle Joe, "I believe I hear it again. Listen there, will you?" At that moment there was a lull in the tempest, one of those strange, short, sudden silences in which the storm-king seems to take breath for renewed fury—and now, undoubtedly, up through the darkness there came a feeble cry—a thin, weak, pitiful wail.

"Oh, men," cried Uncle Joe, "there's a child aboard that craft, the poor little creature. There's a little child aboard that craft. We must save it—we must save it, by the help of God. Give me the end of that rope there, quick! And take a couple of turns of the other end around the tree here. I'll go down and get that child"; and he began to tie the rope securely around his body.

"Let me go, Uncle Joe," said one of the others; "I'm a younger man than you, an' ought to take the risk."

"No, boy," replied Uncle Joe. "God Almighty let me hear its cry, poor little thing, an' I believe He will help me to save it. Anyhow, I'm doin' His work, an' I'm not afeard, whatever way it goes. Lower away handsomely, boys, when I give you the word, and when I pull the rope three times, you'll know I want to be hauled up. Now, then, steady!"

Carefully the brave fisherman swung himself clear of the cliff and hung suspended over the dark chasm. Down, down he went, the men above paying out the rope, inch by inch, slowly and carefully—down, down, swaying heavily in the fierce wind, half blinded by the driving, icy snow, until at length his feet touched the deck, and he turned the light of his bull's-eye lantern around it. Alas! There was little to see; the whole forepart of the vessel had disappeared. She had parted amidships, and only the after part remained, wedged as in a vice between two huge rocks. Hurriedly, Uncle Joe hastened to the spot whence the feeble cry still proceeded.

The companionway was gone, but the ladder remained in place, and down it swiftly and cautiously he descended into the cabin. What a sight met his eyes as the lantern flashed upon it. The cabin was full of water, on which, as it rolled to and fro, floated the dead body of a woman; while high in an upper berth, at the side, saturated, but not yet submerged by the relentless sea, was a little child of perhaps two years old, sobbing most pitifully amid its awful surroundings.

There was no time to be lost, and quickly, yet very tenderly, he snatched it from the berth, wrapped a quilt carefully around it, and regained the deck. Then, giving three tugs at the rope that still secured him, he was swung steadily off the reeling deck, the little one held safely in his strong right arm. Not a moment too soon, for scarcely had he swung clear when the pent-up fury of the storm burst into the gulch with a noise like thunder, and a huge wave, surging upon the remains of the ill-fated craft, wrenched them from their position, and dashed them to pieces against the cliff.

Meantime, swaying awfully in midair, the two precious lives hung suspended. Up, up, up, steadily, slowly, surely, they were pulled, until at length Uncle Joe heard a voice a few feet above his head, "All right, Uncle Joe?"

"Yes, boy," he said, cheerily. "Have you got the child with you?"

"Yes, boy, thank God," he answered, and a chorus of thankfulness came from the men above.

As they reached the top, one of the men bending over while another held his feet, lifted the child from Uncle Joe's arms, and in another moment both were safe. Untying the rope from around his body, Uncle Joe took the little one in his arms again.

"It's no use waiting, boys," he said, sadly.

"This is the only life that's left, and this'll be gone if we don't get shelter and warmth for it soon. I'm going to take it home. Lead the way there, boys, with the lanterns, quick."

With all speed, the return journey was made, and the house was soon reached. Aunt Betsy rose from her knees as the door opened.

"I've brought a Christmas Box for 'ee, Bets, my maid," said her husband, with a strange quiver in his voice, placing the little one in her motherly arms; and then the nerves that had been so long strung to their utmost tension suddenly gave way, and the strong man threw himself on the settle, and wept like a child.

Years have passed, many long years, since that stormy Christmas Eve. Uncle Joe and Aunt Betsy are old and feeble now, and the babe, then rescued, has grown into early womanhood: their more than daughter, the light of their eyes and the stay of their declining years. Yet still, the old man's eye will kindle and his wife's hand stroke softly the fair hair of the girl on the low seat beside her, when at the Christmas season the friends gather round his fireside to hear anew the sad and startling story of Uncle Joe Burton's strange Christmas box.

Three Cheers For the Queen on Citadel Hill

TRUDY DUIVENVOORDEN MITIC

This account traces the Victorian Christmas traditions celebrated by the British soldiers stationed in the colonies each year on Citadel Hill in Halifax.

O n a cold Christmas morning in the late 1800s, the squeaky protest of leather boots crunching on well-packed snow could have been heard echoing against the barracks that surrounded the courtyard on Citadel Hill. Having assumed their position in the centre of the yard, the regimental band would have bravely raised their frost-tinged instruments, deeply inhaled the frigid air, and struck up the first frail note of a familiar march.

The reaction from the barracks would have been almost instantaneous. Everywhere, windows would have been flung open and soldiers dressed only in nightshirts would have reached out and roared their jubilant "Hip–hip–hurrahs!" across the courtyard.

So began a Victorian, soldier's Christmas.

The Halifax Citadel, at the turn of the twentieth century, was a cold, damp, and comfortless home to the 850 soldiers of three Batteries of the Royal Artillery. The meagre buildings that comprised the complex were ill fitted to brave the constant onslaught of the winter winds that whipped mercilessly over Citadel Hill, sending icy fingers of cold through every crack and crevice.

The soldiers on the hill, most of whom were unmarried, lived in groups of eleven to fifteen to a barrack. (Married soldiers were housed elsewhere in the city.) For the young soldiers who largely led an austere and severely regimented existence, Christmas was a time for indulgence and merrymaking. (Indeed, it seems that the government condoned the rampant use of alcohol during the holiday season, and made available to the soldiers great quantities of liquor and spirits.)

The festivities were not limited to a one-day celebration, as is indicated in an 1888 publication, *Six Months in the Ranks*:

> *Christmas Eve and the two following days were holidays in barracks. There were no drills. All the men were busy adorning their rooms; and, to add to their jollity on this blessed day, they received three days' pay advance, with an extra half crown added. All punishments were remitted… cells were cleared, and peace with goodwill were in the ascendant. The only fatigues performed were by volunteer parties who were putting up decorations in the church and the officers' quarters; but these men were rewarded for their trouble by the chaplain and the officers respectively.*

Christmas morning was marked with a colourful Church Parade. Soldiers in full-dress uniform marched to the beat of the regimental band, winding their way to the Garrison Chapel on the corner of Cogswell and Brunswick Streets.

Back in their carefully decorated barracks, the soldiers eagerly awaited what could easily be described as the best meal of the year. Perhaps, to quell their increasing hunger, they might have taken a swig of beer from a four-gallon cask that had been presented to each mess by the officers. Perhaps someone might have dipped into his tin of chocolates, a gift to each soldier from the monarch.

Finally, the bugle call to dinner was triumphantly sounded as a joyous procession of men carrying trays heavily laden with the steaming festive board made its way from the kitchens to the barracks.

To the delight of the soldiers, there was an ample supply of beef, turkey, sausage, roast potatoes, vegetables, mince pies, and other delicacies. There were huge holly-decorated puddings "larger and rounder than cannon balls."

In the cold and damp barracks, the rapidly cooling food was quickly doled out on plates as lips smacked in eager anticipation of the feast. In an attempt to keep them warm, the pies were hastily arranged around the blazing coal fire in the blackened grate of the fireplace that dominated one end of the room.

On one of the carefully made cots sat a polished tray that held a bottle of sherry and a collection of glasses. While the beer and cheap liquor flowed freely, the sherry was reserved for toasting the senior officers whose custom it was to visit the barracks during the meal.

When the expected officers appeared to deliver their Christmas greetings, the men rose to attention, some of them struggling under the effects of the excesses of alcohol. Politely they listened to a prepared speech—the same one that was presumably delivered to every barrack. Glasses were filled with sherry, passed around, and raised to lips as a toast was proposed to the visiting officers.

After the dinner, many of the soldiers proceeded to drink themselves into a drunken stupor. By mid-afternoon, a number of brawls had broken out and the barracks would probably have been approaching a state of shambles. The cells, which had earlier in the day been emptied out in a gesture of goodwill, were again being rapidly filled to repletion.

Those more distanced from the consumption of liquor helped themselves to lemonade and other non-alcoholic beverages. Later in the afternoon, they might have met with comrades around a large Christmas tree in the yard, chatting amicably and perhaps puffing on new clay pipes.

The more adventurous of the group might have donned fur caps and mittens to ward off the cold, and indulged in some sledding down Citadel Hill.

By evening, those still sober enough to do so would probably have gone to a dance at one of the military facilities in Halifax. Many would have retired to their cots, succumbing to a deep and dreamless sleep. Still others could have been found groping their way around the cold, comfortless barracks, groaning and retching miserably.

So ended a Victorian soldier's Christmas. In the days following the holiday season, the military courts would have been at their busiest, issuing the usual punishment for drunken bawdiness: a fourteen-day confinement to barracks.

And yet, even with the excessive consumption of liquor and the general disorderliness of the day, Christmas provided the soldiers momentarily with a rare reprieve from the rigours of a dull routine and a hard life.

Even as the bleary-eyed men returned to their regular tasks and postings, they could take solace in the fact that Christmas, resplendent with a longing for peace and good will, would most assuredly come again.

Uncle Alec's Christmas Pie

ROSALIE MacEACHERN

Times were hard in 1930s Nova Scotia, but families pulled together at Christmas to celebrate the joyous season no matter what. In this story, Rosalie MacEachern retells her father's recollection of a Christmas on an Antigonish County farm, when economic and health worries took a back seat to youthful high spirits.

Christmas always came when my father and his seven siblings were young, but in their old age they marvelled at how it was accomplished. The gifts were modest enough—a rubber ball, a small book, a cloth doll, a rough wooden sled, and on the best of Christmases, a pair of skates that strapped on over bulky overshoes—but the spirit was rich and enduring.

One particular Christmas stood out in my father's memory, and not for the presents it brought. It had been a hard fall of the farm, as on all the farms up and down the South River. Poor crops meant nobody had much extra that year, but there was more at stake for my father's family. My grandmother, always frail, had been sick for two months. The doctor said she needed rest, a scarce commodity for a farm mother of eight.

My grandfather was worried about her and my father, who was the eldest child, sensed it. He had often overheard my grandfather say she had been worked too hard as a child. He had also heard the story of how when they married they lived close by the sea but my grandmother suffered from a relentless cough. The doctor said she would never be well in the damp, salt air so they returned, my father in arms, to the hilltop farm where my grandmother was raised, adopted by neighbours weeks after her mother died of complications of childbirth. Although the neighbours were relatives, they and her father had little time for the needs and fancies of a bright young girl, and that played a role in the kind of woman my grandmother became.

And so December, with its ever-shortening days, came on the heels of fall. My grandmother seemed to get a bit stronger, but only if she spent a good part of the day in bed, knitting, sewing, and darning with her young children buzzing around her while the older children helped as best they could to hold things together. With Christmas near, my grandfather, who could hardly have afforded the expense, sent for Mrs. Benoit, a woman from down the river who was good at practical nursing and better still at the running of a house. With a couple of days' help, he thought everything could be made ready. He was sure a clean house and pantry shelves stocked with baking would do my grandmother's health good.

Mrs. Benoit, it turned out, was just the woman for the job. She bristled with energy and her raspy voice, with its Acadian accent, commanded immediate attention. She had the added incentive of wanting to get back to her own family by Christmas Eve. She swept and scrubbed and hung laundry to dry over the woodstove, clearing curious children from her path at every turn either with a biting comment or a cuff to the ear. So surprised were the younger children by her sharp tongue and flying hands, they soon gave her a wide berth.

Not until she began to bake with a vengeance did they dare to creep closer. As she wrestled pans from the cupboard, Uncle Alec saw his chance, reached round her, and dipped a finger into the batter. She brought the wooden spoon down on his knuckles so hard and so swiftly that all the children scurried to the shelter of my grandmother's bedside.

Bitterly, they railed against Mrs. Benoit while my grandmother tried to soothe them with Gaelic endearments. She told them she did not mind fingers in the batter, nor noisy games, nor small items out of place, but Mrs. Benoit did and Christmas would be here soon so they must be very good and take care not to trouble her.

For a fleeting time they heeded their mother's advice, but the smell of baking biscuits caused them to grow careless again. When the big pan came out of the oven Mrs. Benoit tipped the biscuits onto the kitchen table and returned to her mixing. The children watched carefully until her back was turned and Uncle Alec, judging they had cooled enough to handle, advanced to the table and tossed biscuits over his shoulder to the troops in the rear.

Mrs. Benoit turned her head and roared while the wooden spoon flew indiscriminately. Once again the children fled to the shelter of my grandmother's bedroom, protesting they were always allowed fresh biscuits. My grandmother agreed they had been horribly mistreated, for she never minded their attack on the biscuits, nor their swiped spoonfuls of jam, nor bowls licked clean, but she begged them, as good children, not to trouble Mrs. Benoit with Christmas so near.

So the little ones stayed close to the bedroom door while their older sister tried valiantly to assist Mrs. Benoit and my father worked outside, shovelling snowdrifts and stacking firewood. The restless children might have been better off outside but Mrs. Benoit had no time and my grandmother no energy for the coats, boots, hats, and mitts that were required. Instead, they listened to my grandmother's stories of other children and other Christmases.

Finally, Christmas Eve dawned and Mrs. Benoit escalated her cooking and cleaning. By mid-afternoon everything in the house was done. Truly, the house was as clean as ever it had been and everything was in its place. My grandfather came in from the barn preparing to take Mrs. Benoit home in the horse and sleigh. First, though, he went down to the cellar with two brin bags and a large pot. When he returned there was a roast of salt pork in the pot and the brin bags were filled, one with potatoes and one with apples.

Mrs. Benoit said the roast would make a fine Christmas dinner for her family and that the apples and potatoes would help them through the winter, God spare us all.

My grandfather, who liked his tea "hot as the hinges of hell," poured a cup to fortify himself for the journey as Mrs. Benoit updated him on all the cleaning and household chores that had been completed. Proudly, she threw open the door of the side pantry and began an inventory of her baking.

"Jesus, Mary, and Joseph," she shrieked. "Come here, Joe, and see what the god-damned mice did to my pies!"

Even as my grandfather set down his steaming cup he had his doubts, but he followed her into the pantry. There on the shelves, among the glistening loaves of fresh bread, the perfect biscuits, the fragrant molasses cakes, and the sparkling sugar cookies sat two golden apple pies, each with the rim of its crust eaten away in a perfect circle.

Mrs. Benoit was in a fury, swearing alternately in French and English, for her pies, with their tender crusts and thick fillings, were her finest accomplishment and she was known up and down the river for them.

Dutifully, at her urging, my grandfather got out mice traps, baited them, and set them in a circle around the damaged pies. Then he guided Mrs. Benoit toward the door, reminding her that the light was fading and that her own family would be waiting. Leaving my father and his oldest sister in charge, he urged them to add wood to the fire when it burned low, watch over the younger ones, and keep the pantry door firmly closed.

Mrs. Benoit was still castigating the mice as my grandfather ushered her out into the waiting sleigh. He could only hope the dancing sleigh bells drowned out the sound of the children cheering her departure, for now Christmas, with all its familiar joy, could truly begin.

My father could never remember much about the Christmas morning that followed, only that my grandmother was up and about. There must have been presents, the usual small things, with handfuls of nuts and hard candy, a few squares of fudge, and a piece of fruit to fill the stockings. What he did remember was my grandfather asking my aunt to bring out one of Mrs. Benoit's pies after Christmas dinner.

My aunt, who had grown serious with the added responsibilities of the fall, distastefully placed one of the pies on the table, saying loudly and decisively that she would never eat anything that had been eaten by mice.

My grandfather cut the first slice of pie, looking from child to child. The scent of apple, nutmeg, and cinnamon filled the air as he lifted it from the pan.

My aunt again insisted she would eat nothing touched by mice— mice that had probably crawled all over those pies, back and forth across the top crusts, dragging their dirty tails behind them.

One after another the children sadly turned down the slice of pie my grandfather offered.

"What about you?" he asked my father.

My father had provided Mrs. Benoit with choice chunks of hardwood for the pie-baking and he had dreamed of her pies while he stacked row after row of winter wood in the shed next to the house. Perhaps, he thought, the mice had not touched this one slice. No, it was clear the crust had been nibbled all the way round. But didn't all farmhouses have mice?

Who knew what other food might have been touched by mice and eaten without consequence? And how dirty could a mouse be, living in this ever-so-clean house?

He wavered long enough for my aunt to repeat her comment about dirty tails dragging behind them.

"No," he said reluctantly, glaring across the big table at his sister.

"You're sure?" asked my grandfather.

"Sure," said my father, with the greatest of pain.

"Well, then, I guess it is all mine," said my grandfather.

"What about me?" shouted Uncle Alec, fairly bouncing in his chair. "I didn't say I wasn't eating it. Give me the biggest piece you got."

My grandfather passed him a piece, looking him straight in the eye.

"You don't mind that the mice dragged their dirty tails back and forth across it?" he asked.

Uncle Alec could only shake his head as the juice from the pie ran down his chin.

My grandfather looked at my father again, raising an eyebrow, as if trying to signal something, and then savoured his first bite.

"You're eating that?" my aunt squealed and shivered.

"I'm taking a chance," smiled my grandfather.

My father had sensed something in the way his father looked at him, something that was enhanced by my grandmother's barely stifled laughter. But it was a vague sense of something that did not add up. It did not surprise him that his brother would eat pie nibbled by mice. Alec, after all, had only last week dropped the firecracker through the upstairs heating vent so that it rolled under Allan MacGillivary's chair and took years off his life.

"That young fellow, I tell you now, that young fellow will never die. He'll be hung, you mark my words," Allan proclaimed, abandoning his tea and moving on to spend the rest of the evening with a childless neighbour.

Late that night the younger children were sleeping but my father was lying awake. He heard my grandmother on the stairs and then she came into the room where he and his brothers slept, her husband standing behind her in the doorway, a lamp in his hand. She sat on the edge of his bed to catch her breath and after a minute she thanked him for the work he had done with his father, doing jobs better suited to a man than a boy. She thanked him also for his help in the house, for keeping the younger ones safely out of trouble.

"You should have this before you go to sleep. It could be quite a while before we have another apple pie," she said, handing him a generous slice.

My father took the pie but looked questioning.

"Ask me no questions, but I guarantee you it is safe to eat," my grandmother laughed, turning toward the door with her customary Gaelic entreaty that he sleep well.

For a fleeting second my father saw them both, smiling in the lamplight, looking as they must have looked before their cares rested so heavily on their shoulders. Then he tucked into the Christmas pie.

September Christmas

GARY L. SAUNDERS

Struggling with writer's block and a host of devastating world news one September day, Gary Saunders turns his thoughts to Christmastime and realizes what is so special about the season.

I write these words sitting outdoors in the morning sun at an old picnic table under an ash tree that is in full, if slightly shopworn, leaf. I am supposed to be writing a Christmas piece. But as it is only the eighth of September, Christmas is far from my mind.

One of the quirks of magazine writing and publishing is that monthly magazines must work two or three months ahead—longer with special issues. For a writer this is ordinarily no problem. It's perfectly possible to put together in March a convincing piece on summer gardening or to bang out a story on deer hunting between cold beers at the beach in August. But Christmas, unlike broccoli culture or deer stalking, is no ordinary thing.

And, as luck would have it, I seem to have picked a poor day and place. This particular September day seems laden with distractions. The sky, for instance. Seldom have I seen it wear such a shade of peacock blue. And it is remarkable, I think, how very white are the high cirrus streamers hung across its vault. For that matter it is remarkable how very golden is my golden retriever as he worries the bumblebees mumbling over their late summer shopping among the balsam blossoms. And the crabapples—it seems I have never seen the little scarlet Dolgos burn so bright.

Another distraction that follows naturally on these observations is the distraction of every country place: country chores. It has been well said that a garden is a job forever. I see that the onions need their spears bent down and their shoulders uncovered, to build bigger bulbs. I note too that the raspberry canes are whispering among themselves that I've been slow to prune this year, despite a good crop. Before I know it the netted gems will need digging, and after that the strawberries will want tucking in. And soon the firewood will have to be put under cover.

I would have been smarter to stay indoors at my desk, where I've things arranged so that the only window faces away from chores. Looking out, I can see only the lane, a bit of my neighbour's pasture, and a big sugar maple. Actually the maple has a serious crack that opens and closes in high winds. But that doesn't disturb me any more because I've already taken precautions, with cables and turnbuckles, to prevent its coming apart.

A further distraction, internal but never below the surface, is the matter of the doings of the several offspring of my spouse and me, living their separate lives away from home this Monday, while their father is on vacation writing this, and their mother is on the telephone, building community. The three youngest are at their desks in local schools, too busy coping with new teachers, new classmates, and new topics to muse on Christmas.

In southern Manitoba the eldest is probably squinting across miles of rippling blond grain from the cab of a dusty red combine, while a thousand miles westward his brother is settling into university life again. And their sister is this very week travelling from Montreal to Togo, West Africa, following a dream. Will she think about Christmas at thirty-three degrees Celsius in the shade? Will the three spring offspring get home for the winter holidays, or will this be our first Yuletide without them?

Below that level of consciousness are everyday concerns too numerous and too mundane to bear repeating except that they, too, conspire to crowd out thoughts of Christmas Future. Ironically, among them are the irritations of early Christmas advertising, portents of the onslaught to come. Already *National Geographic* has offered me "the perfect planner for you, your family, your friends."

The fact is we are already planning as hard as we can, and would prefer to leave Christmas unplanned—if we dared. And a book company advises me to "get a head start on your holiday preparations...."

A head start? What is this, a race? Most folks I know are already running as fast as they can just to stay in one place. They certainly don't need head-starters out in front taunting them. That's why I always send my Christmas cards *after* Christmas.

So where in September, amid such common concerns, does the anxious writer, sitting perplexed under his September ash tree, turn in order to glimpse the magic bird of Christmas? For surely a thing so perennial can never be wholly absent at any season—appearances and feelings to the contrary? Like the grass it must surely have deep roots, roots deeper in the human heart than the memory of turkey and tinsel, deeper even than sentimental songs and a fat man in a red and white suit.

One wouldn't expect to find such magic in the media, especially not of late. One of the oppressive features of this September has been the blizzard of bad news—not just the steady rain from Africa and the Middle East, but now the gunning down of worshippers in an Istanbul synagogue, the brutal Pan Am hijacking massacre in Karachi, the Soviet cruise ship disaster, the Lake Nios gas cloud that snuffed out hundreds of human and animal lives in Cameroon, the devastating drought in the American Southeast, two horrific jet crashes, and many more such calamities. These are dark and wintry times on Planet Earth.

And yet, when humankind—Christians, Moslems, Jews, and Hindus alike—celebrate their festivals of light and life, is it pure coincidence that we do so at the very season of the darkest day and the longest night, at the very time when, in the northern hemisphere at least, every summer songbird has fled and every garden blossom is a shrivelled husk? The words of American poet Emily Dickinson come to mind:

> *Hope is the thing with feathers*
> *That perches in the soul,*
> *And sings the tune without the words....*

One thinks of weary Second World War soldiers downing their rifles to clamber from their bloody trenches at that mystical season to hug the enemy for an interlude between the shouting of the guns. Well, if blood and hurt make the best soil for this green thing called "the Christmas spirit," then this year of Our Lord will not lack for blessing. We can be thankful that life in Canada is not so calamitous. If anything, our Christmas is in danger of suffocating under sheer largesse of material wealth. But we have our moments. Last year, on the afternoon of The Eve, I met a friend who hadn't had time to fetch a tree for his family.

"Why not come right now and cut one on my woodlot?" I said.

So we spent a pleasant hour tramping the woods and chatting until we saw the Right Tree.

In the mail a few days later came six poems he had written, including one that said, in part:

> *The first morning*
> *Of a rising joy*
> *The glorious roundness in the soul…*
> *The glorious sun of eternal life.*

Between my friend and Emily, I think they have just about said it.

About the Contributors

Nova Scotian **Will R. Bird** served with the 42nd Battalion of the Canadian Expeditionary Forces in France and Belgium during the First World War, and his experiences as a soldier deeply influenced his writing. His many published books include: *Here Stays Good Yorkshire* and *Ghosts Have Warm Hands*.

Rev. **George J. Bond** was a religious figure in nineteenth-century Newfoundland and wrote a number of stories and legends about early life in the old historic colony.

Born in West Dalhousie, Nova Scotia, in 1908, **Ernest Buckler** studied at Dalhousie University and the University of Toronto before returning to his home province in 1936. Buckler wrote a number of important works while living on his farm near Bridgetown, including his masterpiece, *The Mountain and the Valley*.

Ralph Costello served as president and publisher of the *Telegraph-Journal* in Saint John. A past president of the Canadian Daily Newspaper Publishers Association and the Canadian Press, he authored *The First Fifty Years*, and co-authored with Douglas How *K. C.: The Biography of K. C. Irving*. He died in 2001.

Norman Creighton was born in Nova Scotia in 1909 and lived for many years in Hantsport in the Annapolis Valley. As a writer and radio broadcaster, Creighton charmed Maritime radio audiences in the 1960s and 1970s with his popular radio broadcasts about Maritime life and the natural world. He also created the CBC noon-hour radio series "The Gillans." He died in Hantsport in 1995.

Wayne Curtis is a writer living in Fredericton, whose numerous books include *Long Ago and Far Away: A Miramichi Family Memoir*. You can find him online at waynecurtis.com

Trudy Duivenvoorden Mitic is the daughter of Dutch immigrants who came to Canada through Pier 21 in Halifax in the early 1950s. She successfully chronicled her parents early years in Canada through her book *Canadian By Choice*. She has also co-written *Pier 21, The Gateway That Changed Canada*.

David Goss is a celebrated New Brunswick storyteller. His books include *Saint John Curiosities*, *It Happened in New Brunswick*, and *Only in New Brunswick*. He lives in West Saint John, where he runs Walks n' Talks, a community tour business that introduces residents and visitors to local history.

Rosalie MacEachern is a freelance journalist living in Pictou County, Nova Scotia. A contributor to *Atlantic Books Today* and *Celtic Life International Magazine*, Rosalie also writes a books column for two newspapers in Nova Scotia, and a weekly column for *The News* in New Glasgow, Nova Scotia.

Beatrice MacNeil is a writer living in Sydney. Her books include *Butterflies Dance in the Dark*, *Where White Horses Gallop*, *The Moonlight Skater*, and *A Mouse in the House of Miss Crouse*. Her work often features her own intimate knowledge of the highlands of Cape Breton, its landscape and people.

Kevin Major is one of Newfoundland and Labrador's most prominent writers. He has written a number of bestselling books, including *Hold Fast*, *The House of Wooden Santas*, and *As Near to Heaven by Sea: A History of Newfoundland and Labrador*.

Lucy Maud Montgomery, Canada's best-loved author, wrote numerous books in the early decades of the twentieth century—but without doubt, her masterpiece *Anne of Green Gables* remains the all-time favourite and the bestselling Canadian book of all time.

Hilda Chaulk Murray was born in 1934 in Maberly, a small outport community on the Bonavista Peninsula in Newfoundland, and currently lives in Mount Pearl. She taught at Gander Academy and received her MA in folklore from Memorial University in 1972. She later taught at the College of the North Atlantic and published *Cows Don't Know it's Sunday: Agricultural Life in St. John's* and *Of Boats on the Collar...the Changing Face of a Newfoundland Fishing Community*.

Best known as one of Canada's most distinguished poets, Nova Scotia's **Alden Nowlan** (1933–83) is also one of the country's most enduring novelists and short story writers. His impressive bibliography of works includes *Will ye let the Mummers in?*, *The Wanton Troopers*, and the collection *Bread, Wine and Salt*, which won the 1967 Governor-General's Award for poetry.

Michael O. Nowlan was born in Chatham, New Brunswick. He spent thirty-five years as a schoolteacher, most of them in Oromocto, where he has lived since 1964. He has edited or written more than twenty books, including the poetry collection *The Other Side*, and the Christmas anthology *The Last Bell*.

Josie Penny was born in Roaches Brook, Labrador, to Métis parents in 1943. Her early life was spent moving about as her family pursued a semi-nomadic lifestyle hunting and fishing throughout Labrador. Penny was later sent away to boarding school where she experienced appalling punishment and humiliation. She survived, and attended McMaster University in Hamilton.

Born and raised in Newfoundland, and a long-time resident of Nova Scotia, **Gary Saunders** is known for infusing his passion for the Atlantic provinces into his writing. An artist and naturalist, Gary has published a range of non-fiction titles, including *Trees of Nova Scotia*, *Discover Nova Scotia: The Ultimate Nature Guide*, and his childhood memoir *Free Wind Home*.

Mark Tunney studied journalism at the University of Western Ontario and served for many years as the editor of the *New Brunswick Reader*. He currently teaches in the Faculty of Journalism and Communications at St. Thomas University in Fredericton.

Elsie Douglas VanWart was born in Stanley, New Brunswick, and lived much of her life in Fredericton. She published a number of stories in the *Atlantic Advocate*.

Prince Edward Island writer **David Weale** has been collecting the stories and sayings of the island most of his adult life. His works include *An Island Christmas Reader* and *The True Meaning of Crumbfest*.

J. Keith Young had a life-long passion for photography and taught the craft for a number of years. He lived in Lunenburg and later in Dartmouth but retained a strong interest in the folklore and history of Lunenburg County.

Publication Credits

Bird, Will R. "One Cold Night." *Sunrise for Peter and Other Stories.*
Toronto: Ryerson Press, 1946. 122–36.

Bond, Rev. George J. "Uncle Joe Burton's Strange Christmas Box."
A Christmas Box: Holiday Stories from Newfoundland and Labrador.
Ed. Frank Galgay and Michael McCarthy. St. John's: Harry
Cuff Publications, 1988, 68–73.

Buckler, Ernest. "The Finest Tree." *Thanks For Listening, Stories
and Short Fiction by Ernest Buckler.* Ed: Marta Dvo k. Waterloo:
Wilfrid Laurier University Press, 2004, 212–15.

Costello, Ralph. "A Five-Dollar Performance." *The Price of Honesty:
Life, Laughter and Liquid Lunches.* St. John: Brunswick Press,
2011, 99–101.

Creighton, Norman. "Sending Christmas Greetings," A CBC Radio
Talk. Broadcast on November 28, 1975.

Curtis, Wayne. "Growing Season." *Sleigh Tracks in New Snow.*
Lawrencetown, NS: Pottersfield Press, 2014.

Duivenvoorden Mitic, Trudy. "Three Cheers For the Queen on Citadel Hill" (19th Century Christmas on Citadel Hill). *Nova Scotian*, December 20, 1986, 2.

Goss, David W. "Christmas Past: A Victorian Garland." *The Beaver*, December 1993/January 1994, 4–13.

MacNeil, Beatrice. "A Christmas Journey on a Still, Magical Night." *Nova Scotian*, December 24, 1988, 3N.

Major, Kevin. "Buying A Watch For Billy's Christmas." *Atlantic Advocate*, December 1973, 48–49, 55.

Montgomery, L. M. "Aunt Cyrilla's Christmas Basket." *Christmas With Anne and Other Holiday Stories*. Ed: Rea Wilmshurst. Toronto: Mclelland & Stewart, 1995, 45–59

Murray, Hilda Chaulk. "Feeding the Family." *More Than 50%: Woman's Life in a Newfoundland Outport 1900–1950*. St. John's: Flanker Press, 2010, 181–84.

Nowlan, Alden. "A Call in December." *Miracle at Indian River*. Toronto: Clarke, Irwin & Company, 1968, 29–32.

Nowlan, Michael O. "A Christmas Trip to Town." *Atlantic Advocate*, December 1981, 31–2.

Penny, Josie. "A Joyous Winter." *So Few On Earth, A Labrador Métis Woman Remembers*. Toronto: Dundurn Press, 2010, 225–30.

Saunders, Gary L. "September Christmas." *September Christmas*. St. John's: Breakwater Books, 1992, 103–09.

Tunney, Mark. "Waiting for Santa." *New Brunswick Reader*, December 26, 1998, 12.

Weale, David. "The Eaton's Beauty." *An Island Christmas Reader*. Charlottetown: The Acorn Press, 1994, 17–19.

VanWart, Elsie Douglas. "One Happy Christmas." *Atlantic Advocate*, December 1956, 33–40.

Young, J. Keith. "Belsnickles—Vanishing Race." *Chronicle Herald* (Halifax). December 30, 1960, 6.